PRISONER # 5104

AND OTHER SHORT STORIES

APAR SINGH

This collection of poems is dedicated to the energy that I feel. This energy has liberated me, and given new wings to my imagination. It's the energy due to which art exists in this world, and every artist craves for. Like my previous ones, this work too is dedicated to the same heavenly energy.

This energy has liberated me with its kindness, and inspired me with its hustle. It has helped bring out my courageous side by smearing me with its attitude, made me stronger by killing me, and yet keeping me alive. I have been re-born and re-written in the last few months.

Contents

Preface

Maybe I'm committing a thought-crime as I write down these lines. Anyways, I am happy to finally share this book with all the readers. These stories are based on real life, as I know it except for a little touch fantasy and wilful imagination here and there. Thus, it would be apt to call these stories creative non-fiction.

Writing this book has altered me as a person. I might have not been efficient, and as imaginative or productive I can be, but I tried to give my best. It brought me face to face with my angels and demons. These stories here serve three broad purposes.

Firstly, in order to write non-fiction which is my ultimate desire, I needed to first clear my head of thoughts that are reflected in themes of stories in this book. Secondly, sharing happiness increases it multi-folds and vice-versa. Thirdly, we all can learn from each other's experiences and save ourselves the trouble.

Hence, I have tried to confide in my readers whatever I possibly could, hoping that many will be able to connect with these stories in one way or another.

Acknowledgements

First of all, I would also like to acknowledge *Notion Press for the amazing job that they do*, by providing a platform for self-publishing to independent and part-time writers.

I believe that irrespective of who we are, where we live, or what we do, we all have some interesting stories to share. Some stories are real, some unreal, and others a blend. Stories come from memories and memories fade with time. They tend to bend in congruence with our ever-changing perception. Memory although intangible, is the only real thing that actually belongs to us. And yet we often fudge with it – myself a guilty! So, I would like to acknowledge *people who gave me memories,* although I would like to appreciate a few who gave me happy ones – *like oasis in a desert.*

When I started out writing short-stories, I thought it would be a rather easy and short project. I had no idea that it's hard to keep yourself sane, if you hit writer blocks. I had no idea how difficult it's to write without your muse. I had no idea how much discipline and focus goes into something so creative, even for those of us who enjoy writing. Yes, I do write - I am a poet. *I would like to acknowledge my muse for making me stronger, so that now I can carry on big writing projects alone.*

I would like to *acknowledge Nikki, who nudged me* every time I lost zeal while writing these short stories, given her indifference to my initial writings of poetry. She worked hard to spare me a lot of time for this book, by taking over most of my responsibilities at home. Hope she manages to read the book and find it interesting!

I have put a lot of hours into this book, and it helped me put together pieces of a puzzle that my mind is. *So, last but not the least, I would like to acknowledge myself.*

Prologue

Assumption is the mother of all fcuk ups.

Let us focus on what we could do, rather than what we did not. Let us focus on the times spent together, rather than the voids. Let us focus on the future, rather than the past.

P.S. - I love the shades of your love <3

CHAPTER I

Narrow lane

'Papa do you see a cross-road at the end of this lane? Look at me, see how fast I am going to run.' Ajay said. As he dashed and disappeared down the narrow lane, Arjun flash backed to his own childhood memories. This lane wasn't always narrow, and has a special place in heart. Instead, it used to be an avenue - albeit not a cobbled one, with many guava trees on either side. Towards the end, near the crossroads used to be two java plum trees on either side. The kids used to climb up and eat fresh fruits, and play in the shade. Today, there's barely enough space for a car to move on its shoulders without falling from the verge, into lower ground at sides of an ironically wide farmland. Ajay couldn't wrap around his head as to why the lane was so narrow? He asked, 'Papa why do we have to drive here, as if we're crossing a fragile bridge.' Arjun couldn't respond, there was too much to tell.

Snapping him out of deep thoughts, Ajay came running back and complained with his heavy breath, 'Papa you didn't see me race right? You're always lost in your world.' Comforting him Arjun said, 'I know you're a champ. Since you ran so fast, let me reward you with a good story tonight. Let's go back inside now.' As they entered the gate, crossing the garden and stepped into the veranda, Arjun was flushed with passion. The powerful emotions seemed to grip him, and he felt tears swell up in his eyes. This house they'd just walked in, held the happiest memories of his cherished childhood. To see this place so desolate and forlorn, broke his heart and wrenched his soul. This is where he was born and had spent a better part of his early childhood. Here lived his maternal grandfather aka Nana Ishwar's family, with a few cows and buffaloes in the backyard shed. The place was always abuzz with energy, noise and movement. It was surrounded on all four sides by the family farms, as long as you could see. The kids used to climb up the roof in the mornings and evenings to enjoy the panoramic view. In the late evenings and nights, they enjoyed watching the vehicle lights race on NH-1, or GT road as he likes to call it.

A few days he'd go out with Raj, his maternal uncle to the farms & countryside, holding the radio playing former's favourites, as the tractor tilled the soil in a frenzy. The morning and evening baths used to be the highlights of his day, with cousins joining in and splashing in the tube-well, no less a luxury than a swimming pool and with fresher water. The memories of strolling through the fields, sight of sunflowers, wheat, paddies swaying in wind are fresh like yesterdays. Once in a while, he'd find snakes or snake skin in the fields during trips to his favourite Indian jujube tree. And how can he forget the horror stories of his elder cousin, who dared him to go into the fields at night to pee, while the ghosts roamed around! On the weekends he usually went to his maternal aunt aka Masi, who lived in the city. His earliest memory is from one such days, when they returned after watching 'Hum Aapke Hai Kaun?' on tricycle rickshaws. He'd have so much fun there with his cousins, that he'd feel like not coming back to the village. He would manage to pursue his Masi to send his cousins to village on weekends, instead. What mornings, what days, what evenings and what nights!

Apart from Ishwar's, there was another family of Ishwar's younger sibling, Krishan that lived across the fields in a similar house and had similar sized fields, as if a xerox copy. There was almost no difference in the two families, except that there were no kids at latter's as his children were not old enough to marry yet. This worked well for Arjun, as he had all the place to himself and competition from other kids to share his time and space with. He was the sole centre of attention in that household, he could bathe alone in the tube-well, milk the cow, and what not! He even convinced Krishan to let him use his prized double-barrel rifle hanging in the hall, when he'd be able to lift it. At nights he'd watch classic Door-darshan series like Vikram-Beetal with his uncle, before returning to Ishwar's. Those days power was as unpredictable as love is these days, on and off. Besides backups were unheard of. So, he'd get lucky if the power cut wouldn't happen till the end of episode. On his way back, he'd cross the fields with no lights and as careless he's always been, usually carried no torch with him as well. Post watching the ghost 'Beetal' on television screen, and returning through fields filled with all kinds of animal sounds used to creep the hell out of him. Yet, he was ready to brace the lows for the highs.

That evening, Arjun and his son took a bath in the tube-well after a walk in the fields. As the sun set on the beautiful evening, they clicked a picture of the setting sun. Birds made their way back home, human and machine sounds quelled, as the world slowed down with night-fall. Arjun had bought some dinner on the way, so they didn't have to cook. They had a quiet meal, before going upstairs to enjoy some clear starry night time. Ajay looked at the vehicles which appeared as small dots of lights zooming across NH-1, just like his father used to as a child. Meanwhile, Arjun poured a few pegs in memory of the old days before lighting a smoke to ignite his 'burning fire'. Before going to sleep they came out in the garden in early spring night of March, a little cold, a little silent, a little cosy, without much wind around.

'How long are we here for, papa?' Ajay asked. 'How long do you want to be here?' Arjun asked. 'As long as you wish to be, but I must say I find the place a bit lonely.' He said. 'Well, we can leave tomorrow. But as I said earlier in the day, let me tell you a story before you go to sleep.' Arjun replied and Ajay was all ears. 'You see, this world is a weird place. I know it's not for you now, but as you grow up you'll see it. And the weirder part is that you'll begin doing some things too, so that you don't seem strange to the others. And if you do choose to be yourself, you'll be seen as weird!' He stopped as Ajay intervened, 'Isn't that strange?' Arjun continued, 'I'll tell you what's strange. People forget they're mere mortals and that they're never in possession of anything. They forget they're never in control. They forget they're not selfish innately, but in trying to conform end up living a life of deceit - to themselves!' He took a brief pause and looked at Ajay. He still seemed to be intently listening. He wondered how a kid who's just seven putting up with him, when people of his age cannot.

Arjun continued, 'You see the story here is a similar one. Do you see that house on the other side across the fields?' Ajay nodded in agreement. 'That is the house of a brother. A brother who got so selfish and full of himself that he raised his head against his elder one. He was ready to raise his hand too by the way, only if he could.' he stopped as Arjun raised his hand. 'But why would a brother do that?' He asked but Arjun ranted on, 'He allied with other like-minded 'family foes' to force his brother's hand into doing things he didn't want to and cough up land that he didn't have to. He's the one responsible for us to drive a narrow line to home. So full of greed that he cut the trees on sides, even dug the road at his side, sparing not even an inch though he owned vast lands.' He stopped, anger simmering somewhere in his eyes. Arjun asked, 'Then why didn't we widen our side of the road?' Arjun replied, 'Well, we did try. You see the more we widened, the more he'd dig again to claim more land as his own. In the end, he just wanted to give a hard time to Ishwar. There was no choice, but to leave it as a narrow lane.'

Arjun asked again, 'But why would a brother do that?' Arjun took a deep breath, 'I can't say for sure Ajay, because nobody really knows or tells the truth – it's all a shade of grey. Each side have their own version of truth, so truth is quite subjective depending on 'vantage point'. But if there's one thing I can tell is that it's about possession. Now possession isn't a bad thing in itself, for everyone's entitled to some. But when the avarice sets in, and selflessness is bartered for acquisitiveness, values are lost, false injustice are perceived and no compromises are made. Adding fuel, the fire is a sometimes a manipulative wife'. Ajay asked, 'So where's everyone gone now? Why this place is left so desolate?' Arjun said with a sigh, 'Ajay everyone wants peace, but don't want to fight for it. Everyone wants love, but don't want to sacrifice for it. Everyone wants happiness, but don't want to suffer for it. Everyone wants pleasures, but don't want to work for it. Everyone loves a good life, but don't have the guts to live through it.' Ajay said, 'Can you be clearer?', Arjun came down from his philosophical bandwagon, 'You see, it's difficult to stand for the things that matter to you. It takes guts, sacrifice, pain and hard work. 'This place matters. It offers you a good life - clean air and water, fresh food and milk, a healthy lifestyle with peace, happiness, and love. You see love can't survive in absence of peace and happiness, without a feeling of fulfilment.'

He continued, 'Yet, people have left here for the rat race of an urban life. All men wish to provide and care for their family. So, sometimes one has to do things which they otherwise wouldn't want to, such as leaving the adventurous countryside life for a monotonous city one. Usually it's for the kid's future and wife's happiness, and there's nothing wrong with that per se. But do you get the point I make? You go with me where I go, you see what I do and feel how I do. Tell me, is it worth it?' Ajay replied, 'I guess I know what you mean. There's always a way to keep things you love, and make time for them. There's always a path that takes midway and in order to keep others happy, we shouldn't die inside.' His reply assured Arjun, and with a pat on his back, ruffled his hair, and kissed him good night. Next day in early morning, before they left Ajay wanted to have a final run. As they went outside the main gate, Arjun again stood at the end of narrow lane, seeing him dash in distance and smiled. He thought to himself, 'I just hope there won't be any narrow lanes in this world because of Ajay. May the kids find fruits and shade of the trees!'

CHAPTER II

Erstwhile

In 455 BC, there was a major sandstorm wiping out entire dominions in erstwhile undivided west Indian region of Sindh. As nature's fury poured, realm's people and institutions were devastated. As fortunes needed to be rebuilt and towns were to be resurrected, Shankar Rode was chosen to lead the able bodied men, by the elders of the city council of Rodi. He turned out to be an exceptional leader, who could motivate the masses and direct the lords. The hard work put in by people over the next couple of decades paid off as the dominion was back on its feet, rather doing better than ever. Rode's dominion spread across Western India till present day Rajasthan. With time, it turned to a nation state and his dynasty would rule over these lands for the coming eleven centuries, via forty-two kings in succession. This is until a coup by the prime minister of last ruler in 620AD, that would effectively end the linage's rule.

This would not turn out so well for the Indian sub-continent, as the western frontier was left in weaker hands. Within next two hundred years, the state would fall to Islamic invaders, leaving the gates open for them to attack rest of India. As cities were lost, Rodes moved their base to Gujarat & Rajasthan and later to modern day Haryana and Delhi. They turned a mercenary tribe and continued their fight against Islamic invaders. With time they eventually settled down as peaceful farmers across the Yamuna river. This brief tale is about our protagonist Shankar's tryst with destiny, his going from a misfortune to leaving behind a legacy, with his deeds still recounted in ballads in afore-said regions. These extraordinary events that transpired in his life had a major role to play in his quest for a better world. Of these events, his love story is worth a remembrance.

Shankar fell in love with a woman of eternal beauty, named Surath which literally means face. She was born to a jeweller in the capital city of Rodi, leaving everyone amazed with her brilliance and her beauty. One summer evening, when Shankar was walking down the city market, he chanced upon Surath. It wasn't love at first sight, but admired her fierce walk, charming talk or god knows what. Nobody would call Shankar a romantic, the word 'romance' meant nothing to him. Well, that was soon about to change. One autumn afternoon, she called out to him, 'Do you mind buying some jewelry for your loved one?' 'No, thank you, I don't have one.' He replied. She persuaded, 'I suggest you have a look, there could be something that catches you eye.' There was a magnetic pull in her voice, one he couldn't resist.

He picked up an anklet and asked, 'How much for this one? 'That would be one silver coin.', she replied. She spoke like flowers showering from her lips, and he hoped that she'd not stop. She too felt an urge to continue the chat. Soon the topics shifted from one to another, and they both ended up conversing for some time. He bought the anklet and bid her good bye, until next time. The stars burnt brightly that night, and the waxing moon hung beautifully in the sky. As Shankar lay on in his cot at the rooftop, he was perplexed by Surath's thoughts. He'd never felt such a connection with anyone before and tried in vain to figure out his emotions. Back at her home, Surath too wondered about him, and looked forward to meeting again.

Since then, whenever Shankar would cross her shop in the market, he'd have a strong urge to go and talk to Surath. Surath on the other hand began wondering, why he never came back after that first lively conversation. One day as he was crossing her shop, he stopped in his tracks as she watered the plants at shop. He asked her, 'Would you mind if I join you for a lunch?' She agreed with a playful smile, as she excused herself to wash hands. The lunch went surprisingly well, the best he'd ever had. That day onwards, their friendship took off as Shankar would often visit her as they began to bond over time. Sometimes they'd meet up for lunch, sometimes for a break, and sometimes they'd just have a small talk when he'd pass by. Shankar always looked forward to meeting her. Soon Shankar thought of expressing his feelings to her, but didn't want to ruin it in haste. He wasn't sure though if she knew his intent, or if she had the feels him. In the middle of a harsh desert, she was an oasis for him which he couldn't lose.

He would bring gifts to lift her spirits and appreciate her. She too didn't disappoint him, ever. Smitten, he'd write poetry on her and would often ask her, 'Did you like my poems?' and she'd laughingly say, 'I did, but still can't figure out if I am the inspiration of your poems.' In the middle of these harsh winters, she was a bright sunshine for him. Shankar felt their friendship was too platonic, wanting more of her, and to know her better. One serene evening, he asked her, 'Would you like to go out with me?' She nodded, 'Sure, we'll go soon, I'll let you know when we can.' They eventually fixed a date and it went well. Under the stars they dined and wined, and shared little secrets. They'd go out a few more times, until one such night while walking her back home, Shankar clasped her hands, looked into her eyes and said 'I've wanted to kiss and hold you tight. I had the courage and will but the moment was never right.' He leaned in kissed her good bye.

The next day when they met, she looked at him with lobbying eyes and he whispered to her, 'You are like a fantastic story with hidden truths, waiting to be found by one with patience and a will to discover them.' She spoke softly, 'I don't claim that your thoughts have been completely overwhelmed by my influence, but seem surely compromised by it.' As they planned for a rendezvous, Shankar's friend Eerav informed him of being summoned by the council. Knowing that he'll be out of town for the next four days, they parted half-heartedly, unaware of fate's plans. At that same hour in nearby dominion Sana's king Ani, was gifted a painting of a woman with most illustrious beauty, and he was roused with desire as he wondered the whole night about having her. Next morning, he called the person who'd gifted him painting, 'Who is the lady in the painting?' He replied,' All I know is she's from Rodi, but I can check with the artist I brought this from'. Ani said, 'Please do my friend, it's a matter of life and death.' As his friend took leave laughing, little did he knew what was to follow.

The morning after, Ani came to know of Surath and by evening he'd sent messengers to her father in Rodi, asking for her hand in marriage. Sana was a resourceful state and the family's riches were envied across subcontinent. By the following morning, Ani's messenger had brought his proposal and valuable gifts to Surath's father. Being unaware of her daughter's love-life and desirous of seeing her as a queen, he immediately said yes. Ani had put forward a condition, that since it was his birthday one day hence, so he'll bring the marriage party on the same day. When Surath came home in the evening, she chanced on the presents and inquired them. She was left aghast upon hearing what had transpired behind her back.

Meanwhile, she went to check on her friend Bhuv, asking him why he'd sold the painting to someone, when she could pay his ask price. Bhuv was remorseful, and asked for her forgiveness. She then consulted with her most trustworthy friend Rani, who said, 'It's best to tell your father about the whole thing, even if he can't do much now. I have a friend Daivat, who's a messenger for the council, and he'll carry your message to Shankar for me.' She agreed with her, but chose not to tell her father. He couldn't do anything now, for he'd given his word. As Shankar's best friend Eerav came to know of Surath's marriage from Daivat, he knew things could turn ugly and at once informed all well-disposed people in the council and the forces. Knowing Shankar, he knew, that he wouldn't give up on her.

Ani's birthday came and the marriage party entered Rodi. Ani was welcomed at Surath's place and she left for the Sana in a palanquin. By this time Shankar was already on his way back, twenty miles from Rodi's gates. Since he'd anticipated that they might not be able to make it in time, they chose a path taken by travelers between Rodi and Sana. Eerav gathered a backup force and quietly followed Ani's party out of Rodi, keeping a safe distance. He wondered what Shankar had in mind as he and Ani weren't the types to give her up without a fight. Ani asked his men to take a break and freshen themselves up, as the weather was a little harsh. Suddenly, out of nowhere Shankar confronted Ani's men and asked to be taken to him. Ani and Shankar went to a nearby temple. As they stood under an old banyan tree, Ani heard his story and was gripped feelings of loss, jealousy and uncertainty. He was overcome desire of having Surath.

He spoke to Shankar, 'She is my wife now, whatever her past had been. And what about people at Sana? What would they say, I can't let her go?' Shankar tried to reason, 'I agree, and I'm sorry that things turned out this way. But she won't be able to love you, the way she does. It'll ruin and bring only despair to both of you. So, for the sake of Sana and its people, please think of this as an unfortunate mistake and let it go.' In trepidation, Ani pulled his sword from scabbard and charged at Shankar in a frenzy. Shankar had anticipated this, but he didn't want violence. So, he rushed back to his camel and gave a shout to his men, who he'd instructed beforehand to find Surath and being her to him. They charged at Ani's men and a fight ensued in the middle of the desert. Meanwhile, Eerav and his men came out from hiding, and in a matter of minutes the fight was over. Half of Ani's man lay dead, and rest were captured.

Surath was found, and Shankar pulled her up to his camel. Ani and his men were cornered up, bounded and gagged. On the way back, he thanked Eerav for lovingly said, 'What I'd without you?'. On reaching Rodi, the news spread like wildfire and reached the city council. Shankar was summoned to explain himself, which he did - forthrightly and fearlessly. Luckily for him, they were indulgent. So, he and Eerav were let off the hook without much trouble. Meanwhile, back in Sana, Ani was drinking the poison of humiliation. A message was sent to Rodi, that even though trade would continue, their military alliance against foreign invasions did not hold anymore.

For Shankar and Surath, it was time to celebrate and meet each other. Taking her father's blessings, they tied the knot at the old

Shiva temple. They lived a doting life for the next two decades, having six children. Meanwhile, Shankar helped fortify Rodi, built new alliances, expanded territory, always remaining wary of Sana. In early forties, a target of court conspiracy Shankar lost his life in an accident. None knew for sure, but it was rumored that Ani's spies were behind Shankar's fall. His eldest son Rudra succeeded him, and rest is history.

CHAPTER III

Unhinged

With thuds at bedroom's door, Arun woke up from slumber. His new-born sister Anita began crying, and mother Kamini, exhausted from the day reacted slowly. Thud, Thud, Thud! 'Who's it?', demanded Kamini, knowing who it was. Thud, Thud, Thud! 'Open the door or I'll break it anyway!' came a heavy voice. 'What for?' she retorted. 'Open the door and I'll tell you!' Clank! As latch unhinged, Arun's drunk father Shashi rushed towards Kamini, pulling her out of bed. As Shashi and Kamini fought, he felt odious. Post shouting and violence, Shashi left and Kamini sat crying on the bed. Barely five years old, Arun felt powerless!

'Come out of bed Kid', a thirty-one-year-old Arun wakes up his son for school. He's got his hands full with two loud & eccentric kids – a boy Arjun and a girl Avni, and spiteful wife Kavita. He has gone with the flow, in a month they'll celebrate seventh anniversary. 'I need to shop for marriage. When do we go to the market?' she asked. 'Tomorrow, after office hours', he replied. Arun is not in a happy space. He had hopes, a sense of pride and belief. All that changed when he got married early, and under pressure. In his naivety, he had a kid within two years, demanding his time and space. 'I want a divorce with Kavita.' he remembers telling his mother one year ago. He never went through with it, and ended up with another kid.

He's been under-employed all along his career, which now spans almost a decade. He's changed more than seven companies in this time-frame, disinterestedly doing odd jobs. 'I'm done working to survive not thrive!' he says, slamming bag on floor when back from work that evening. He can't even write, feeling shackled, his life gravely lacking love and inspiration. Kavita is a home-maker, and takes good care of daily chores. However, he never wanted a maid, but a partner! She too wanted more, 'Why did I marry a guy who didn't even own a home or car?', she would often say in despair. Kavita said, 'Why can't you get a well-paying job or move abroad, like blah, blah!' His hopes from future are dim, and another job alone can't fix his life. The damage done seems irrevocable, and out of hand, like he's lost his youth, energy and desire. He just pays the bills, handovers what's left to her and however unlikely, hopes it'll all get better.

As a kid to impress the girls, he often asked Shashi, 'Papa when will you buy me a jacket?' No answer. He got by winters wearing mom's hand-knitted sweaters, buying his first cool jacket with his first pay check, fifteen years later! When five, he cajoled Shashi, 'Papa when will you buy me a bicycle?' No answer, again. He got one ten years later, when his friends were riding motorcycles or driving cars. Nevertheless, he took it out and a car rammed him, leaving him with plastered wrist. Shashi said, 'I knew this would happen if bought you a bicycle.' Arun replied, 'Why wait all these years?' In college, he requested, 'Papa buy me a motor-bike.' No answer, yet again. He bought one five years later, by then the girl he wanted to take out was gone with someone. We are not financially, but a mentally poor nation! Arun would never do this to a kid, for wealth is skills and happiness, and he knows the pain of being forsaken.

Arun still has trouble in coming to terms with the world. He what Shashi could've done, for him to not wait for years for tiny things – maybe a few less drinks, maybe not. Instead, all he ever got was scolding, never any appreciation, a smile or praise. The irony being that Shashi himself complained of his childhood. At night, he sneaks into the washroom to smoke, becoming a daily ritual now. As he smoked looking at himself in the mirror, he uttered, 'Kill me, today!', looking a decade older than his age, lacking inspiration, and energy. He's taken to drinking from occasionally to casually, short of tippler. He fears that if he too will gulp down a 750 ml bottle some day? Will he too become like his father? Living nearby home town, Arun isn't keen on visiting family, since he doesn't feel at home and the memories don't help much either. No one, ever showed real love or concern towards him, an outsider - he was always away first hostel, and then job.

Arun was a reluctant drinker at first. Drinking revolted him, the cause of all misery. He wondered when Shashi he would've sipped the first pegs? He's heard at thirteen. Shashi would purloin liquor from grandfather Ajit's bottle. He first saw him drink at age four, at night in the guest room, where he used party with friends. A few weeks later, when Ajit visited he spilled the beans. As he mixed cola in drink, he'd innocently said, 'Papa too drinks this black water, you know?' What are we but our memories? On a sweaty summer night when he was five, ignorant of worldly matters, Arun requested Shashi, 'Papa it's too hot! Let's go for a ride.' and surprisingly, Shashi agreed. He enjoyed riding, so every time Shashi tried turning back, he'd prod him to go a little further. Soon, they reached a house where lived Shashi's foe. He got down, and there was a big scene. Arun was shocked and repented. Later, a cop dropped him home, in the dead of night. Till today, he blames himself for what had transpired.

Earlier, Arun would mostly drink occasionally with office colleagues or fortnightly at home with Kavita. However, his drinking has picked up pace lately, turning first into a weekly and then bi-weekly ritual. He now prefers drinkers and smokers, often finding them more open, fun and tolerant than those who don't. However, he steers clear of those leading a life of falsity. For such people behave differently during the days and nights, and with outsiders and insiders, in short are hypocrites! Shashi was an example in the case, and Arun has come to stand anything is life, forgive anything in life except – hypocrisy. So, while making new buddies, he looks for two things – one, do they openly accept that they're a drinker and two, if their disposition remains un-wavering after a few drinks. If it gets even better, they're for keeps!

'No man, I won't drink today. I'll just come for company.' Arun said to his friend on call, the next evening. He intermittently quits drinking to keep a check on his lust, for he fears turning into an addict one day. There's an incident, that makes him fear it. One cold winter evening, when he was eight, Kamini held little new-born Anay in one hand with a ladle in another, preparing Palak paneer for dinner. She hummed in a jolly mood, stopping as Anay began crying. As she calmed him down, upset with commotion and reeking of alcohol, Shashi barged into the kitchen and began hurling abuses and throwing things around. Upset with this, she protested in resentment, and he furiously slapped her, several times! She couldn't even resist as Anay was still in her arms. As he left the kitchen, she sat on the floor crying and said, 'What have I done to deserve this?' Arun recalls the vexatious scene, of Anay wailing as his mother wept, wiping off the vermilion smeared on her forehead. Arun felt sadness!

Unaware his own future would be replete with sorrow, he was brought back to present, hearing Arjun cry, as Kavita hit him. 'Never beat the kids! Don't take out your anger on the weak!', an upset Arun intervened. What followed was a monologue of bitter and scathing words, he couldn't bear. At thirteen, back home in summer vacations, he felt strange vibes. As he over-heard Kamini' s conversation with his Masi Sujata, he was repulsed from Shashi. Apparently one night, Kamini refused Shashi's advances. Angered and teeming with alcohol, he tried to shove a knife into her abdomen, leaving a bleeding palm and a fractured thumb. Soon, one night when his parents were brawling, Arun thought enough was enough! He came outside, and could see some neighbors' shadows in the windows, while some others stood at their doors. No one dared say or do anything, but watched the show, cowards. At nine, their small town was engulfed in darkness, as he entered the police station. Ashamed of what he was to say, Arun felt embarrassment!

As the inspector was absent, so he went up to a SI and said, 'Sir, my father's beating my mom at home. This happens quite often and is disturbing for us kids. I need you to help before something unfortunate happens.' And told him the address. SI didn't even look up and pointed towards a sergeant, 'Bring a written application and give it to that guy.' He replied, 'Sir, I haven't got any paper or pen on me, as I came here in a rush. You need to come to my home right now!' After an eerie silence, they all went back to their work

– doing nothing! He felt like a ghost, was he was troubling them? He overheard that the inspector was drinking in his quarter. The cold response baffled him, as he headed back. Now, he couldn't go to home either, since Shashi would be waiting to welcome him at the gate. Therefore, he spent the night at nearby Shiva temple, with mosquitoes feasting on him. The system is deaf to the weak – the children and women. Arun felt like renegading!

Five years later, while Kamini was visiting maternal home, Arun stayed back for his tuitions. As he stood in the porch one afternoon, enjoying stormy weather of heavy rainfall from the skies, the lightning strikes and the rumbling of clouds. Slam! In a flash, he could see his pinkie finger split into two. The door behind him was forced shut by a gust of wind, and his finger crushed in the hinge. Shashi standing at gate, heard him shriek in agony and flinched, saying, 'Oh, what've you done.' He was worried less for the injury, and more about the trouble of going to a doctor. Arun felt unloved!

That night, as Kavita seemed upset on some petty issue, Arun went to bedroom to find some peace. Though, he prefers women who're a wee dram-atic, he's repulsed by ones who don't know when press the kill switch. When it didn't come inside after some time, he came out to check on her. There she lay teary eyed on the floor, an empty whiskey bottle rolling beside her. His heart sank with pity and anger and asked himself, 'What did I ever do to her that she creates such scene? When and where did I wrong myself and her?' He lifted her up, laying her in bed. Their marriage reeked of unhappiness and unfulfillment.

While asleep, his dreams take him to flashbacks, 'Get lost!' shouted Shashi at Arun who'd returned that evening and had come to greet him. Aged twenty-three then, he had failed at business he tried after quitting first job. Shashi sipped his drink in the living room, not sober enough to listen to any spoken word. He didn't advise or offer to help in any way. In fact, he seemed happy in Arun's misery. He wakes up in morning, and remembers how he was being ill-treated all his life, until he took the high road and made himself loud and clear.

Off-late, he's brawled with Shashi over his ruined childhood, with Anay for his idiocrasy, with Kavita for a ruined marriage and Kamini for always teaching him to be tolerant. As he becomes more resentful and indifferent towards life with each passing day, spending dark evenings in the corner of a room sipping poison, is he now following the footsteps of his father?

CHAPTER IV

Prisoner No. 5104

What does it mean to be imprisoned? A correction facility isn't a requisite, as we can be behind invisible bars at our home, school, or workplace. What's worse than being physically restrained? to be confined mentally. We're prisoners in our own minds, moving from cell to another. Lately, Vijay can't figure out whether his life sentence is getting better or worse, feeling more trapped than ever, all of his own making.

Today was his last high school board exam, and his last day at the boarding school. 'If I score 80% in 10th, you'll allow me to come back', he'd made a pact two years back with his parents and is sure of same happening. He's spent seven years here, yet is happy to leave. It's liberating, but feels drippy too. He'll continue to love and hate the place for the rest of life – it's loneliness, sadness and eerie peace. He was reckless, limitless, a spitfire and an extrovert when first came here at the age of nine. Today at fifteen, he's changed 360 degrees, owing to different people he met and stayed with, apart from all the rules that he had to follow. His high hopes from the future come at a cost - of leaving his old friends behind, who've stuck with him through thick and thin.

When eight years old, and lively and full of wonders, he loved flying kites on rooftop. As one hovered high in the sky on Teej, he twisted and turned it at his whims and fancies; a feeling of pure pleasure, power and excitement. He often roamed town lanes, playing with kids from known-unknown neighborhoods, tearing movie posters from walls to decorate his room. He lived, breathed, watched, listened to, and believed in Bollywood and cricket, a typical small-town boy! However, he has nothing to show up for it, like his other interests pursued in later life. 'Did I give too much of my time to things that didn't matter?' He now asks himself.

Ever since his sister, Shalini had arrived three years back, he was mostly left to his own devices. Only, soon his grades dwindled, as he was having a gala time. Soon, another sibling, Tej was born two years back and he was now almost forgotten, which he didn't mind at all. 'Vijay often skip meals, and mostly stray outside home.' Abha would tell Ravi. Sometimes, his principal had to drop him in his car from school, when rickshaw wouldn't come and none at home picked calls. This will continue for lifetime, with his father Ravi being an ATM, albeit one that only pays school and tuitions fees.

Ravi's a friend cum mentor Satish, also a government employee, had three kids. Two of them of Vijay's age, and he got them both admitted to a boarding school, and prodded Ravi to follow suit. Ravi asked Vijay, 'Would you like to go to boarding school?' Vijay replied in affirmation. He was a kid, and the idea excited him. But his mother, Abha refused. Ravi had tasted blood, he wanted to get rid of Vijay, a nuisance, and there wasn't a better way. Eventually Abha too acknowledged that she wasn't able to handle three kids, and agreed to send him to the gallows. Both convinced themselves, that it was best for Vijay as he'd have a better. This was a turning point in his life, a point of no return!

So, Ravi and his friend Sandeep, owner of a local business, decided to get rid of their trouble-some sons. Vijay left with Sandeep's family for Dehradun, where they stayed with a relative. In admission test, he got stuck wherein he had to write five lines on 'Best Friend'. A lady teacher came up to his desk and asked, 'What is the matter kid?' He replied, 'Hi mam, what does best friend mean in Hindi?' To which she smiled and said 'Pukka Dost'. He quickly wrote five lines and left the room. The lady would be his class teacher later on, and vastly influence his life.

Hostel life shaped him, making him who he is - for better or worse. In primary school, the maids aka aayas took care of the kids. Back then, he didn't brush at nights, nor did he wear slippers or undergarments. He learnt to make his bed and use locker. His belongings were now a small trunk, with his roll no 5104 and a hold-all. On weekends, they'd would watch English movies on cable TV, a privilege back then. Vijay began playing all kinds sport and take part in drama besides other co-curricular activities. Molding self in many other ways – to survive, thrive, learning something from every friend and foe.

It took him some time to settle down, but he turned out to be quite adaptable. Soon, he was in junior school. On weekends, the schedule was same except for the school and timings. 'Hey Vijay, it's alternate Saturday, let's someplace new in the city, I'm bored of cinemas.' said Kuldeep. 'Yeah, we're rich today. Aren't we?' Vijay replied, referring to 100 rupees, each student got. Other alternate ones, were lonely but productive days, and in hunger pangs he'd often miss home. If the sun was out, he'd sleep in the garden or under the trees at playground. Boarders eagerly waited for TV, with a packed hall. They could speak to parents, if they called. Or, they could write letters back home. 'I yearn for freedom.' He'd often say to his friends, for he was missing what his friends back home did not. When vacations came, he was often the last one to leave for home, waiting eagerly wait for his parents to come. Instead of coming themselves, his parents usually sent an acquaintance to pick him up. This went on for five years, until he reached senior school, and could go home alone. He'd submit a fax from his parents, take travel money and catch a bus to Meerut.

In winters you could see the snowclad mountains of Mussorie from the school playground. 'Come here, take this!' said Sandeep, as he splashed freezing cold water on Apar in senior boys bathroom. They used to bathe twice every day and the icy cold winters, often gave him a running nose. 'Bloody, the chimneys aren't firing!' Vijay screamed. Post bath, he screamed, 'Who picked up and used it?' looking at his wet towels and found the undergarments missing from stands. He couldn't ever bring himself to do it! It was so common, that he learnt to ditch them altogether, a habit that stayed. There was some fun as well, that came along with risks. He and a friend, managed to make a duplicate key to TV room for cricket and Sharapova's matches. Sometimes they'd jump glasses lined boundary walls, to eat noodles and momos. The physical punishment on being caught was severe, added to embarrasment for first timers and rustication for repeat offenders.

Some teachers leave a mark on a student's lives. From primary school, some indulged his mischief and took care of him like a guardian. Few, molded him into learning English while others ignited his interest in arts. In junior school, some acknowledged his leadership skills. Some, encouraged his interest in literature, when not many were interested. On hitting puberty, he couldn't find any other outlet, thus finding solace in reading. He would immerse himself in and began discovering world in a library.

Vijay turned a cricket AC, he day he watched India rout Australia in 1999. Indian kit from World Cup in 1999 still remains his favorite. In class six, he got selected for the junior school team. But, all tournament he sat in extras, despite being a handy all-rounder. The following year, he was included in playing-eleven. It was a T-20 format in 2002, six years before IPL made it a norm. They bowled first, and he took 2 wickets in four overs and 22 runs. One might call it a decent performance, except that of these runs, fifteen came from wide balls! It wasn't his day, but was sent first down to chase a small total of 88 runs. He hit the five runs on two balls, before getting LBW on the third. It was the sad end of his brilliant cricketing career! His coach Reddy, was so furious that he never trusted Vijay in school team again – be it cricket or otherwise. Despite being a chess champion for three straight years, he never got to represent his school or district.

Sometimes, hormones got better of him and his thoughts wandered from Algebra to Cleopatra, not even sparing his teachers. Mostly, all he could think of and see was - sex. 'Chadhti jawani is airing, let's go Ajay', Vijay would say to Sunil in excitement, listening to the remix songs that played in hall. 'Nothing's better than kaata laga!' he replied. From morning to night, he was often up, up and up, and even reading science books could arouse him. That is until, he found the secret weapon, the reliever of all anxiety – self-service! Soon, the stand was filled with clothes with stains resembling fevicol and toothpaste. It wasn't easy to fizz in the dormitories at nights, for the beds would shake, when someone shook. The bathrooms were tricky, as the door latches were rarely intact. So, in the evenings, he'd stay behind in the class on the pretext of studying, and he did study hard! The boys' and girls' hostels were separate so there was hardly time for the sexes to gel up. They got together only during day time - at school, and evening preps. The day-scholars were rather free to explore real world.

He hated Mathematics. It's not the subject that's good or bad but the way it's taught. Yet, he managed to do well, thanks to the tuitions that Ravi made him take during breaks. Those days JIL presentations were just beginning to add some life and color to classes. He wished to pursue commerce and economics, Ravi thought otherwise and wanted him to be an IT engineer. In those days Java was taught on the blackboard and screen time was limited to half an hour per week for two kids per system, lol! Besides, there were no tuitions available to boarders. He then tried to take economics as optional subject, but in vain for Ravi denied permission to school. He then picked home science as an optional, hoping Ravi would not know. The next day, Ravi made a special telling him, 'Cooking and cleaning is for girls, Vijay.'

Hostel had limited food options, and bland food. For Apar, variety and taste are what life is, and the standard menu bored him. So, every year, when mess secretary would change, he would chase them revising the menu. He found his hinge to survive in Sambar-rice with vegetable served on Thursday's afternoon. On merciless weekends, especially after home-food was finished. In late nights, when hunger bit, he with some friends would sneak out, and unlock mess with the hairpins to steal some rotis and eggs. The rotis were then fried with ghee into parathas to fill their starving bellies. The annual ritual of looting the canteen, on a random day close to the end of academic year kept the school authorities on toes.

It was the show and pride of unity at senior hostel. For the rebellious boarders, it was like avenging the unjust world around them. Consequently, the guards frequently did rounds of the place. However, the heist would always be successful. The loot would range from everything from cassata ice creams, to shoes, literally leaving an empty canteen. Following day, the manager submitted his bill to the administrative officer, eventually getting reimbursed. The bill was divided equally amongst the senior wing. The rowdies were rounded up by warden, to no vail. There efforts to find a whistleblower were vain too, for the hostel was not a kind place to deserters.

He'll miss it after all! Or maybe not!

CHAPTER V

Limerence

The boarders were on way back from mid-term break, in the Himalayan foothills of Yamnotri, when Rani took one of Karan's earphones. Handing it back, she teasingly asked, 'Is this what you listen to?' He replied 'Yes'. Looking out of the bus, he wondered what she thought of boys who listened to romantic songs. In retrospect, he should've asked her. He was a romantic fool, the ones who never speak up, never dare. But we are, what we are, or can we change? Maybe we should be our real selves, until a soulmate crash-lands onto us. He felt shy walking up a girl and tell that he likes her. Maybe there was none who could make him a man. Besides, he's too slow, and only a girl of patience and strength could bear him.

Karan liked Rani, and began to follow her in class, preps, playgrounds and on evening walks at the quadrangle. In those old school days, limited exposure meant hard feelings. One day, she confronted him, 'Why are you following me? What is it that you want to say?' He was at a loss of words and couldn't say anything. Instead, that evening in prep class, he wrote her a note 'I love you'. She read the note with a smile, saying, 'You are crazy, Karan!' before crumpling and throwing it out of the class window. After that day, neither of them talked about it. At the end of academic year, he vividly remembers her last day at school, the gloomy grey skies of March. With almost all students having already left the campus for their homes, he wandered like a lost soul around the desolate campus. And when she left in a car with her parents, he came back teary eyed to the dormitory, wondering if he would ever see her again.

As Karan moved to class nine, his friendship with Ananya grew. After Rani had left, they sat together in the evening classes. As they began spending time together, gradually some mutual feelings began to develop. However, unlike Rani she already had a boyfriend from a senior class named Sachin, so their friendship remained platonic. On his last day at school, when she came to bid farewell. In her eyes Karan saw and felt from her ways that, had he stayed back, they could have been something. Two years later, he had an entrance exam at Dehradun, and on the way back he went to meet his old friends at school. It was then, that his friend Abhishek told him about her. Karan knew, Abhishek had always liked her and was jealous of their friendship. After Sachin had left, Ananya became his girlfriend, and he boasted how he gave her a deep French kiss. He didn't know what to feel or how to react.

Karan's in full party mood on his third annual college fest. All friends are raring to go, with some vodkas in their bellies. He hopes to meet Saina today, a junior. She's a sweet, comely, lively and a stout girl. She was a well-off, and exposed to the latest in tech. 'What's your WhatsApp number?', she asked once, 'What does that mean?' he had replied. Back in 2011, he carried an Intex mobile worth 2000 rupees, which his mom had bought him after much persuasion, from her pocket money. Yet, she liked him. He mulled if they could have a little dance and then go out for the night. He's kept some vodka in his room, in case he needs to leave in a hurry with her.

So, once the friends clicked a group picture, he made his way to the dance floor in the quadrangle where DJ was playing. As soon he got into the groove of electronic music, his eyes meet Kajal's. 'Till when do I have to see her? Hasn't she wounded me enough already? When she showers him with her affection, why do I wish to kill myself?', he thinks to himself, while acting like he doesn't feel a thing for her, as if he's moved on. He joins Shruti, until her boyfriend takes away, moving on to Roshni, until she gets a bit shy and finds himself dancing alone. As he turns to his left, he finds Kajal dancing next to him.

Karan couldn't believe it at first, for this must be a mistake or maybe she didn't see him here. But, the very next moment she moves in front of him, dancing to the beats. He thinks to himself, 'Wow! is this girl for real? How can she be here, after all I've been through.' Maybe she's forgotten him in entirety, for they last spoke two years back. What the hell he went through! When they broke-up, his eyes couldn't have been more honest. Didn't she see herself in them, when she left – that he'd fall and hit rock bottom. Yet, she did leave him, right? He saw Shashi, her boyfriend standing afar, looking at them and wondered what's going through his mind right now. God only knows how much Karan despises his luck – good or bad, only he could tell.

'Does he know what he's got, like I do? Does he make her feel her safe in his arms, like I would've? Does he treat her right, like I would've? Does he kiss her often with the zeal, like he would've? Well, maybe even better for she chose him, and left me in agony.' he thinks. His self-esteem hit a low, again! and had taken two years to heal. Karan's afraid of falling in love again, for he won't be able to make it one more time. 'Is she here to rub salt in my wounds? Is she just having fun? Does she want to feel good by knowing that he still feels for her?' he kept on thinking as he danced. Then, he stopped and looked into her deep eyes, one he loved. He was not able to figure out much and turning to his right, left.

He could've told her that after all these years, he still felt for her. He could have kissed her then and there to make her his own, and it may take a few more years for the day to come which goes when he wouldn't think of her. But this is not how he works, and this is why nothing works out with him. He might die of pain, but won't spare words on something obvious. She left him high and dry. So, if she had any feels, he needed to hear it from her lips.

On the way out, he saw Saina with her friends. He went ahead and said 'Hi!'. 'Hi!' she said smiling, as always, but with a rather surprised look, for she was always the first one to approach him. 'Did she sense that I'm a bit drunk?' he wondered. But he now already in the pool, so he better gets himself wet. He bluntly asked, 'So, would you like to join me for to me tonight?' Now, there are subtle or funny ways of asking a girl out, and he kicked himself for being so unprepared. His lack of experience was not of much help either. She replied, 'Sorry, but I am busy with my friends tonight.'

He only said, 'Okay' and took her leave. One, for he was a miser and no good with words, especially when it came to girls. Second, he didn't want to say catch you later or something on these lines because the train had passed. That was the end of their short, little friendship. He was done for the night, for good!

He came out of the college gate and took an auto for his room. He did what a loser like him would do on a night like this, what losers do every night – he switched on his laptop to watch a movie, and forget all the misery. The story of his life, a sad one. In the morning, he tried to make sense of last night. As she flashed before his eyes 'Not her again!', he said to himself. Next room, his classmates sleept soundly, lucky bastards! Never been in love, lucky guys! When together, he fooled around, not move past holding her hands. And when she left, he didn't try enough, not showing courage and persistence to follow it through. His life would've been much sorted, if instead of over-thinking had he actually done something. Instead of over-thinking shouldn't he have just worked it out when he had a chance? 'Maybe, it was my stupidity that stopped me. What world do I live in? She came to him, even as her boyfriend looked on.' He thought. He could've talked, instead of second guessing her intentions.

They first met in the first semester, when his classmates Jasmine and Shruti, called Kajal to help with a group assignment. She walked in with a smile and said, 'Hi!', and Karan smiled back at her. Later, he asked Jasmine, 'Can you help fix up a meeting, like a movie or dinner with Kajal?' She agreed, alerting him, 'Shruti is her elder sister, so be discreet.' Over next month and a half, they met often in evenings at college, went out for a few dinners and movies. However, he never got alone time because Shruti always accompanied her. Yet, her eccentricity and joy de vivere kept him going.

He looked forward to meet her, look into her eyes, listen to her thoughts and hold her hands. Little did he knew that she was losing interest. You look worried', he asked her the evening before they left for winter break. 'I've lost 8000 rupees!', she replied. He didn't have that much on him, as he had mistakenly broken the ATM card that his father had given. He told her to tell the truth to her parents. Soon they parted. During the break, he asked, 'How are you?' 'Fine', she replied. Karan asked, 'What's up?' 'Nothing, just hanging with some friends.' She replied. Karan replied 'Cool! You didn't call even me once?' 'Hey, I am busy and got to go.' she replied and the line disconnected. Karan said, 'Okay' as he looked at Aman, who was laughing at him.

Back in college, Aman came along to check out his college at Hyderabad. Karan called and told her, 'I want you to meet my school friend.', 'Okay,' she said, but she didn't show up. Next day he called her again, despite Aman stopping him. She said, 'I can't meet you. I am focusing on my studies and not looking for a relationship right until third year.' He was taken aback, and said, 'Hey listen, let's not discuss this over phone. Let's talk face to face.' She said, 'I don't want to meet.' He was broken, and said, 'It's all right and I get it. But remember, not only you leave me, I am leaving you too.', his voice choking up.

Next day, they left for Bangalore where Aman's sister stayed. When back alone, he again asked Kajal to meet him. She came down-stairs from the hostel, to the lover's spot near the canteen. He looked at her like a prisoner looks at freedom, before he goes for the gallows. They both greeted each other, but none spoke a word. In that moment, he acknowledged that it already over and he walked away.

When after third semester, Shruti shifted back to Kannur, within three months, Kajal had a boyfriend. Hearing of it, Karan felt as if lead was poured into his ears. To keep himself occupied, he went back to his own dark world, which only made it worse. He'd naively assumed that she'll come back to him, not knowing he had nothing for her to come back. He would remain old-school, unaware of the outside world which had moved on, where relationships were altered by social media. A lot has changed since, but Karan was never a part of that story!

CHAPTER VI

Transient

It had been three months since Kajal had dumped him, and Karan had begun to lose perspective. He had lost interest in everything, winding himself in a cocoon. He decided to change, grow, and invest in himself. If he were to ever fall in love again, he wanted to be a better lover. He changed his room, room-mates and wardrobe. He deep dived into music, smoking and intoxication. In decay and destruction, he found growth. Being low & slow, he kept cool, calm and patient, subduing his nature. He'd heard that LSD alters the mind, making one meet their angels and demons, but could never try it. Anything that doesn't kills makes you stronger and wiser.

'Good morning!' said Vedant, stuffing a joint into Karan's mouth as he woke up. At lunch time the room-mates would come back home. 'Suck it up Vedant! Karan please order some parathas from Golden Leaf' Atharv said, handing the bong. Few days Apar joined, others he denied, preferring not to be slow and hazy during college hours. Post dinner Neeraj would serve dessert, 'Here's a submarine for the deep-divers.' The highs of smoky days were so low! Karan was an average student now. 'Had I been in engineering I'd have got better grades than this,' he said to himself, looking at last semester's results. Subjects in a fashion college like garment sewing and pattern making, were a pain you know where. His group assignments were based on friendship and not merit. Thanks to individual assignments, mid and end term exams, he continued to be at-least a six point someone!

He rebounded on Pria, a great dancer with an alluring smile, and an hourglass body. Also, she was his close friend Sourav's crush, and they'd split for almost a year, until the buddy love was revived over a bottle of beer at a friend's place. An evening while high, he rang up Pria. As they were talking, Sourav called and he switched call. 'Bro! I'm in the canteen and the girls are having a gala time, overhearing your conversation on speaker phone.', said Sourav. That was the end of Pria! Besides, he wasn't in love with her. Next semester, she committed to a guy that baffles them to date, but as they say Love is blind!

Love is a feeling, and can't be forced upon anyone. But, then one always falls before the another. Maybe, Karan never really wanted love in the first place for the sake of it, and waited for one who could make him go astray. He looked for some depth, maturity, intensity, flamboyancy and a bit of drama in a girl, a mix so rare that it got him nowhere. He was okay to be nowhere, but not forever! He admired a few girls like Kavita for their beauty, but none who could draw him enough to put an effort. By third year, it was too late, as his mind had altered and his heart was already an island floating in a sea, far from love lands.

'This weekend, let's cook our own food.' Vedant suggested. Karan couldn't cook, so he said, 'I'll get the ration from store and do the dishes.' Atharv was a Delhiite and had an elder sister, a great combo for success at love. His roommates' girlfriends visited in the evening. Later, as the couples latched their doors, he went back to his room, watching screen before jerking off and going to sleep. One such night as he lay down to sleep after getting high, something weird happened. He could feel his heart beat aloud, as if it were in his hands, seeing the universe revolve around him. That night he promised himself this – 'If I survive tonight, I will never overdo it again!' Karan had known for some time that he was going astray, when he went astray looking for an ash-tray one night!

Not that he always had junkie roommates. Joining college, his father dropped him to a boy's hostel, as the college didn't have one for males. His roommate was Varun, a studious classmate. He found his next room-mates in Sourav and Manish, who stayed at the same hostel and shifted to a flat by the end of first semester. Manish was four years older, and became his life coach, and drinking buddy until dropping out of college. Karan's technical knowledge at the time was rudimentary, not even knowing what a pen drive or hard disk was. Sourav stepped in as his 'Tech Guru', helping him create his first email-id - karansinghawesome1@gmail.com.

One evening a visibly upset friend Manvi, his classmate Aman' girlfriend knocked at his door. She came and sat quietly, as Karan waited for her to say something. He asked, 'What's wrong? All okay?' She kept quiet as she got up and locked the door. He asked again, 'Tell me what's wrong?' She blurted, 'He's not faithful, you know. He's been talking to girls all and fooling me all along.' Karan thought for a while and said, 'I know. But he's my friend like you and I can't do much about it.' They both had been friends since the first day at college, often seen together in classes and canteen. She was the only girl he went out with, having fun, but it was platonic. Sometimes, he felt being more than friends, but then she was Aman's girlfriend with her weird smell.

There was a strange silence, as he looked into her eyes. He was lonely and she was pretty. He wanted to kiss her on the neck, moving all the way up to lips and undress her. They were alone and, no one had to know if they did it. He instead said, 'Manvi, I like you. I know what you're saying is true, but he is your boyfriend. You've been with him and eventually you'll go back, and I don't want blame of taking your advantage at a weak moment.' Once, she was calm he escorted her out of the room, and went to sleep. The next morning after he had self-serviced himself, he wondered if he did the right thing yesterday. He went on with his chores, re-collecting his initial days at college – the city tour, fresher's night, etc. etc. He and Manvi used to be a quasi-couple, always together. His classmates Barsha and Natasha tried to get close to him, who like others felt incomplete without a boy/girlfriend. Then Aman, a Mumbai urbanite came in with tricks and ways, which Karan - a small-town boy could never compete with. Manvi eventually gave up fight, agreeing to be his.

Towards the end of third year, a comely batch-mate Ravina, common friend through Sourav would often chat up. He didn't like her, but he didn't hate her, as it was somewhere in between. She was a kind of a girl he would fall for, if not a bit too healthy. Still he was open to 'let it flow', and they met on campus sometimes. One

Friday night she called him, 'Can I come over? I won't stay long, will be gone in the morning.' As always, he was forever alone, and didn't mind company. So, they lay down in bed to see a movie, kissing, caressing and cuddling. Next morning, she left saying, 'I'll be back in evening.' He knew that if he does it, he'll get attached even though she wasn't exactly the girl of his dreams. He got desperate by evening and decided to give it a try. She called him in afternoon asking, 'I am coming at room in evening. Can we you go to the temple?' He could only mutter, 'No.' Going to temple with a girl is like eating gol gappe with her, something very sacred, an epitome of romance. Temple and gol gapping, can be be done with only someone very, very, very special! And that the end of Ravina!

During the college placements at Delhi, Karan felt that he had wasted his precious college years. Almost all his friends settled for what best they could find, exploring love, relationship and sexuality. Meanwhile, all he did was explore himself, owing to his high standards, and never getting into a relationship for the sake of it. All along, he thought that, he'll find the right one, and he'll know when he does. While waiting for an interview, he chanced upon a petite girl Rina, from Kolkata center. He walked up to her, 'Hi! you're really pretty. I couldn't stop myself from talking to you.' She gave a shy smile. They chat up for a while and exchanged phone numbers. He wouldn't get placed until a month later at the fourth round in Mumbai campus. The time in-between was tough on his self-confidence, as not getting placed made him doubt himself. He found himself unprepared, and messed up few opportunities, just like his college life.

Once he got placed, and back at campus for the last semester, he called up Rina. 'Hi' he said. 'Hi! How are you?', she replied. 'Great, it's nice to catch up.', he said. And soon they were regularly talking on the phone. He began to wonder, if she could be his girlfriend. So, one evening he asked her, 'Hey, I really like talking to you, and the way you are. Can we be more than friends?' She replied, 'I already have a boyfriend, and I'm not a virgin.' Karan was taken aback not because she wasn't a virgin, but why she talked to him, if she already had a boyfriend. He asked, 'Why didn't you tell me before? Does he know you call me?' She replied, 'It's complicated. We've been together for several years. He is the guy who took my virginity. It's mostly about sleeping together' To this he replied, 'Who cares! Can't you end it with him then and be mine.' She replied, 'It's not easy, in fact unlikely. Maybe, with time I can.' He replied, 'Either you stop talking to me, or stop sleeping with him.' He didn't want to be a stopgap. Karan was naïve to navigate waters of love oceans. It was the end of Rina!

During his training days at first job, the trainees would often party till late at night. He liked Mihika, and Sukriti liked him. Mihika already had a boyfriend, though she was reluctant to accept it. One night, as he excused himself to the washroom, Sukriti followed him in the heat of moment. 'Hey, what are you doing here?', he asked jokingly. She switched on the tap, and then closed it. Soon, they were kissing passionately. She seemed a bit too high, he felt it was better to stop, and they got back with everyone else. That night, she stayed with him, in his bed. They made out, and slept cuddling.' Next day, when he woke up, he saw she was bald at some places in head. No wonder, she often wore caps. Meanwhile, she developed strong feelings for him. So, he began avoiding her, looking to end it. She then began asking his room-mates and female colleagues to persuade him into talking to her. He didn't, for he did not want to break her heart. But, in hindsight he should've given her closure, and it's a guilt that'll stay.

Shikha, a colleague of Karan's, had caught his eye when he was engaged. She was smart, attractive, independent, and beautiful with a lovely smile. They sat close by and used to get along well. However, he never fully opened up to her. Engaged is not serious! Apar didn't knew that at the time. Also, she was close friends with Shashi, his old-time love Kajal's ex-boyfriend, and now a colleague and a good friend. It was funny that the guy got two chances, when he got none. Shashi, eventually had an arranged marriage like Karan would later. Only Karan would have gone through, and maybe that's why he never got the girl. They want something else but do something else, always!

CHAPTER VII

2,750 Beer

'Urvashi the four beers we drank, costed us 2,750 Indian rupees each!' Arjun said with a laughter. She was furious over what has transpired the previous night, but couldn't help smile back. Yesterday, on their way back home from a mall in Mahadevapura, Arjun had said, 'It's hot today. Let's pick up a bottle of for the evening.' As they rode close to on a liquor shop on the road-side, she suggested, 'Can we instead go to a bar tonight?' Unlike him, her suggestions were not flexible, they were subtle orders. Besides, she occasionally went out, so he thought what the hell. 'Okay' he agreed.

In the evening, reached Koramangala, the place with best bars. It was not their usual hangout area, but Arjun wanted her to try a new and better place. After having two beers each and some food at a bar, they left for home post 10 PM. He was somewhat familiar with the routes and hide-outs of traffic police in the area. In his last three years at Bangalore, Arjun had rode back home drunk many times, without any trouble. 'Hey, hurry. There cops are holding up the traffic.', Urvashi said. It was already past ten and they were in a hurry to go back home. A hundred meters or so, there was a for drink and drive checking going on.

She nudged him to speed up, but a motorbike in front, just wouldn't let them pass. Not wanting to rouse any suspicion, he didn't push hard. Arjun hoped that seeing a family, the cops wouldn't stop them. But, a middle-aged cop stopped him, saying, 'Blow into my face.' Smiling devilishly, he took away the bike keys from the tank. Next, he asked him blow into a pipe. Arjun blew, hoping for the reading didn't show up, and it didn't. The cop asked, 'Blow again', nothing came up. His face dropped, and just then another constable walked up to them. He seemed to know the fix, making Arjun blow multiple times in a row, until the reading came up. Arjun obliged, and soon their eyes turned greedy as if they'd seen gold, and asked them to get down. One took the bike and vanished into nowhere. They now stood on the roadside, as the other vehicle went by.

Arjun knew it was time to try bribe the constables. So, he approached one leading the pack, and requested him to let them go. He said, 'I'm with family, and I had had only had two beers, I'm perfectly in my senses.' The cop turned a cold ear, he didn't care. Arjun then sked, 'Sir, please tell me how much you need to let me go?' '5,000 rupees' the cop replied. 'What?', he said. He expected something like 500 rupees, unaware of the sky-high fines that had come into force recently as per the revised traffic rules. He asked, 'Sir, what is the fine for drink and drive? '10,000 rupees.', the cop mockingly replied.

He stepped aside, and took out his phone to re-confirm. The cop was indeed, right. He went back and said, 'Sir, I only have 3,000 rupees right now with me. It's a good amount. Please take it and let us go.' 'There's an ATM nearby.' said one. Arjun said, 'It's 3,000, take it or leave it.' But the cop didn't budge, and said, '5,000 or fine.' Arjun now boiled up, 'Give me a receipt and I will pay the fine.' Their faces could tell, they were not expecting it and asked him to reconsider. He then said, 'Please take me to the sub-inspector', without whose presence they couldn't levy a fine, but was nowhere to be seen. A cop complied to his request, and escorted him to SI. There he was, sipping whiskey behind the boundary wall alongside the road! Arjun walked up to the middle-aged man and said 'Hello', making him flustered.

The constable apprised him of the situation, and he plainly asked Arjun, 'So, will you pay the fine or give them what they want?' He replied, 'Sir, they are asking for too much. I am ready to give 3,000, but they won't take it. If I need to give more, then I better pay the fine.' It seemed to hurt the SI's ego. He asked his junior to fine Arjun and give him a challan. As the challan rolled out slowly, Arjun saw his precious 10,000 rupees vanish into air. He felt repulsive toward the system, the leachy, blood-sucking system. The money could have been used for so many things, like buying a ring for his wife, a bicycle for his son, paying rent or school fees, etc etc. Instead the money would go to government coffers, strengthening this very sick system.

Arjun was officially a criminal now. He always wondered if criminals were really corrected in India. He doesn't know much about the jails, only the traffic violators, e.g., if one is caught riding without a helmet, shouldn't they be made to buy a helmet, rather than paying a fine more than the price of the helmet itself! Isn't this looting the common citizens? Since the surveillance system with the cameras on roads had come, there's been much inconvenience. The other day, he was reading in a newspaper, that recently a person preferred to leave his scooter with the cops, rather than paying a fine, as the fines were more than the value of his vehicle. As that person went home crying, didn't anyone see his tears, his despair, how helpless he was. It's was parlance with, the hen that lay golden eggs, until butchered!

Another day Urvashi had persuaded Arjun to take her along to the market, as he was leaving for an errand. On way back home, traffic cops stopped them for no reason - like many others, who looked hassled. Arjun wondered why he was stopped, he was riding properly, both wore helmets, and had all the paper work in place. He questioned, 'Why I am being halted here for no reason?' The cop didn't answer, instead just punched in the number on motorbike plate. Suddenly, his face lit up like a kid. He said euphorically, 'See, you have a fine to pay, 1,000 rupees.' Arjun repeated, 'Why did you stop us in the first place?', to which the guy had no answer. He made up one, 'It was a *geo-tag* alarm that buzzes when a vehicle with unpaid fine passes nearby.' 'What? Why did you have to punch the motorbike number then?' Arjun said, bewildered. 'Anyways what is the fine for?' he continued. The cop said, 'It's for talking on the phone while riding.' Arjun had once checked his phone while halting at a near ISRO signal, waiting for the green light.

Anyways, an irate Arjun took the receipt, and began walking back towards the road, when he heard the SI calling him. 'Come back. Give me your license.' he said. Arjun questioned, 'What for? Haven't you already fined me and taken my bike? Where is it by the way?' The SI seemed roughened up. He repeated, 'I need your license.' Arjun handed it over and asked, 'Now, please tell me where is my bike and how do I get it back?' The SI replied, 'Go to the court tomorrow and pay the fine. Then come back to Koramangala police station, and collect the bike after submitting receipt of challan payment. Arjun asked, 'And my license?' 'That too. Show me you RC, by the way', he replied. Arjun took it out, with one hole already punched in it. The SI smirked, 'You must be glad that I am not punching a second hole here. Three punches and an RC become invalid'. Arjun said nothing, and began walking away. The SI said, the most niggling thing possible at the moment. 'Give me 500 rupees, and take your license back right now.' Arjun was rather amused, and smirked, 'I was ready to give you 3,000 rupees and you didn't take it. Now after you have levied a fine of 10,000 rupees, you're asking me for 500 rupees?" The SI went quiet, visibly disturbed by his response. He was behaving like a waiter, who has the nerves to ask for a tip, after one pays the bill with service charges in a restaurant.

The following morning, a female lawyer called him up. He asked her, 'How did you get my number?' She informed him, 'Every morning, the cops upload the offenders list on the city traffic police website.' He took a leave from office, and along the way, his landlord dropped him to the court at 10 AM. He met the lawyer there and handed over all documents, along with 11,000 rupees - the fine and her fee of another 1,000. Sitting idle outside the court, he met the doctor who too had haggled with the cops the night before. They were given 12 PM slot, and had plenty of time to kill and began talking. Over the next two hours, Arjun learnt about cool Airbnb places in Karnataka and Tamil Nadu, to hang out. He told him about becoming a doctor, his best and worst experiences, and how here eventually migrated to Australia. He was back only for a week, and see this is what happens to him, enjoying a true Indian experience or homecoming, so to say!

At 12 o'clock the station names were called in an alphabetical order. By 12:10 PM the offenders began pouring into the court premises. There were so many, from different backgrounds, ethnicities, and regions. It was a 100% male crowd, and made Arjun wonder about lack of female participation! They were asked to queue as up their police stations that issued challan last night. Soon, they began going inside as per their station names. The court resembled one in movies, but was somewhat smaller in size. All they had to do was to go to a desk, and when being called by their names (again in alphabetical sequence), had to sign a paper pinned to the desk by a court clerk. *That was it!* It was the fine that counted, rest was all drama. Next, they collected the challan receipt from the office outside court. A whole day for this. *A whole day for this!* This seemed like just a small example, of how a nation loses its productivity.

They both took a cab to the Koramangala police station. After reaching there, they had to wait another hour for the constable to come. And when he did arrive his attitude was no less than a prime minister's. He took them to a parking lot adjacent to the station. The doctor got his car keys, examined it and left bidding good byes. But, Arjun's bike was nowhere to be seen, and the constable kept asking for him to wait. He then took Arjun on a motorbike, near to the spot where he was fined last night.

He told Arjun, 'Wait here for some time, and I'll be back.' After twenty minutes or so, he was back. When Arjun saw his bike, the first thing he wanted was for the cop to get off it. To his relief, all parts were in place and once satisfied, he looked up and asked, 'Where did you park my motor-bike last night? You did not park it the designated area, right?' The constable blandly replied, 'It's none of your business. Your bike is perfectly okay. Now, let me click a picture of yours with the bike as a proof of handover.' Arjun let him click the picture, and asked, 'Where is my license?' to which he replied, 'You'll have to come to the station for it.' Arjun said, 'Aren't we coming from there.', realizing by then, that they won't give it unless given their alms of 500 rupees.

They had no idea that they had only a duplicate color copy of his license. 'Never mind', he said with a smile, as he ignited the engine of his motor-bike, leaving the cop bewildered.

CHAPTER VIII

Recluse

Shivam and Raman, best friends since school days, had met after a long gap. As they were talking about old days, Raman said, '*There never a mess too big to get out of!*'. Shivam could only nod in agreement. In life, sometimes things do seem to get out of control, but only the chances one takes, makes them become wiser and build resilience.

Shivam was reminded of the Chemistry externals viva day during class XII boards exams. It was a bright spring morning, with upbeat vibes. There is so much else, that can be done on such days, then being in a class. Shivam felt that he had done better than he thought would. As he waited for his turn, the visiting faculty excused herself to answer nature's call. It was then that he saw Vaibhav, seated in the next row, scribbling answers from a book. Shivam easily falls to temptations, for he is impatient and greedy. He couldn't stop himself and went up to his seat to asked what he was up to.

Vaibhav smiled, and said, 'Can't you see? I'm writing the answers.' Although, Shivam felt that he didn't need to cheat, but gave in. So, he said 'What the hell, can I check my answers too. It won't take long, as I've already written down the answers. I will be done in a minute.' Little did he know, what was to follow. He took the plunge, and just when he was leaving for his desk, the invigilator barged in. She caught saw the book and acted so furious, that Shivam was left perplexed. She shouted, screamed and threw fits! Years later, when he was a married man, and lay in bed after a fight with his wife, he would figure out that this is how some women behave.

She rounded up the two of them, and summoned the subject teacher at chemistry lab, where practical was going on. More than the possibility of having to repeat a year, he was upset for leaving his teacher embarrassed in front of an outsider. Not that he particularly liked her but for she was his teacher. He always had a certain respect for teachers, maybe for they helped him be a better person, or maybe it was because they filled the void of elders in his life. Or maybe, he felt they weren't treated justly by students and schools. Despite working hard for something that mattered the most – the future of a nation, they were a subject of ridicule and under-paid. *They got too little in return, for what they gave to society!*

They both were then asked to leave the room, and their answer sheets were taken away. In that moment, Shivam had a weird realization. He actually didn't seem to care about failing the exam, or getting a back year. *He had in-fact been failing all along*, and it was a feeling of liberation. He mulled that even if he failed, he can start over again. It was something he couldn't do if he keeps going down the same unidirectional life path, set for him by others. A life of his ways and dreams, was taken away bit by bit since childhood. There were so many other things a person can do apart from studies. He didn't want to be an engineer, or scientist or whatever nerds do. He always felt pressurized studying dull subjects like science and computer applications.

Also, the whole hum-drum made about this thing, him feel like a criminal. And that too *didn't seem to bother him!* He had no shame or guilt, albeit a tad remorseful. He sat there in an empty corridor, imagining for himself an alternate career as a criminal. They were then asked to report at the principal's cabin, where the receptionist asked them to call their parents, and ask them to come to the school as soon as possible. Vaibhav rang up his father first, who probably left right away. Meanwhile, after thinking about it for fifteen minutes, Shivam mustered courage to call up his father. For one, he wasn't sure that he would pick up the call and two, even if he did pick up he won't come. However, he rang him up, and wasn't he right? His father, Tej was visibly upset and refused to come. Although he knew it would happen, yet it broke his heart. He felt alone.

Soon afterwards, Vaibhav's parents arrived. They were very concerned and met the principal right away. What is it about the only child? Whatever rabble they rouse, their parents always seem to forgive them. They tried to calm Vaibhav down, which obviously wasn't needed, as he was already calm. It was Shivam who needed someone to talk to. He soon left the school, without saying anything to anyone. He felt blank on his way back to his uncle Shyam's place, where he stayed.

There was an unusual stillness and peace of mind that Shivam felt. He realized that day, that he actually had no one to turn up to in times of crisis. Not that he had never felt it before, but had never let himself acknowledge it out of fear, fear of knowing that one is alone. He had been harboring false hopes all his life, and felt that he didn't need them anymore. On reaching the house's doorstep, he didn't feel like entering it. It was rather meeting his uncle who was just a different version of Tej, that stopped him. He imagined him making fun of the whole situation, and him in particular, as always. He was in mood for bland humor, and decided it was better to be alone. So, he instead took an auto and went to his classmate and friend Rajiv's home. A spacious and peaceful place, where no elders would bother him with their prying eyes and questions. Rajiv was son of a single working mother, who was at mostly occupied.

Upon reaching there, rang the bell. Rajiv opened the door but didn't say anything, for there was nothing he could say to make Shivam feel better. He then, climbed the stairs going straight to the rooftop, wide open and with a lot of sunshine. 'A better choice definitely!', Shivam said to himself. He laid down on the floor with no mattresses, no pillow, and no sheets. He had never needed them and slept in the sun for straight four hours. Once awake, he liked the peaceful and sound sleep so much, that he decided to stay there for the night as well. In the evening, he listened to some music on Rajiv's desktop, before going back to sleep, slumbering through the rest of night.

Next day, he woke up very fresh, having slept so well after so long. He first took some time to process as to why he was there in the first place, and what had happened the day before. He then left for his Shyam's home, and reached there in about half-an hour. He rang the bell, and Shyam's daughter Himadri opened the door. She was a sensitive girl, and could always tell his mood from the look on his face. She too didn't say anything, as he went upstairs to his room. There was no one else home, as the couple were both lecturers and had gone to college. He didn't feel like doing anything, and there was no one to talk to. Even his mother hadn't called to check on him, and neither did he expect her to.

So, he lay down and recoiled in his bed, staring at the side wall. Then he rolled up, stared at the ceiling and decided it was better to go back to sleep. He got up in the night, and quietly had his dinner. He didn't tell his uncle anything about what had transpired at school. They all looked at him uneasily as it was unlike him, for he always brimmed with energy, no matter how much life sucked. So, the next day when he woke up, he could feel that there was no more sleep left for him to catch up on. He freshened up and went outside to have some bread-omelet at a nearby *thela*, before leaving for Raman's place.

He and Raman wandered around for a while in the neighborhood, before leaving for Vaibhav's place, who lived nearby. Raman gave him a call, 'Hey, me and Shivam are standing outside your home.' Vaibhav soon came out, and they chatted for a while. As they talked, he reassured Shivam, 'It's sorted out. Don't worry! My father has pulled some strings.' As they parted, Shivam didn't knew how to feel - to be happy or sad. *It was all the same again.* He will now have to lead a study-work-marry-die life. Was he dead inside?

Shivam and Raman, best friends since school days, had met after a long gap. As they were talking about old days, Raman said, '*There never a mess too big to get out of!*'. Shivam could only nod in agreement. In life, sometimes things do seem to get out of control, but only the chances one takes, makes them become wiser and build resilience.

Shivam was reminded of the Chemistry externals viva day during class XII boards exams. It was a bright spring morning, with upbeat vibes. There is so much else, that can be done on such days, then being in a class. Shivam felt that he had done better than he thought would. As he waited for his turn, the visiting faculty excused herself to answer nature's call. It was then that he saw Vaibhav, seated in the next row, scribbling answers from a book. Shivam easily falls to temptations, for he is impatient and greedy. He couldn't stop himself and went up to his seat to asked what he was up to.

Vaibhav smiled, and said, 'Can't you see? I'm writing the answers.' Although, Shivam felt that he didn't need to cheat, but gave in. So, he said 'What the hell, can I check my answers too. It won't take long, as I've already written down the answers. I will be done in a minute.' Little did he know, what was to follow. He took the plunge, and just when he was leaving for his desk, the invigilator barged in. She caught saw the book and acted so furious, that Shivam was left perplexed. She shouted, screamed and threw fits! Years later, when he was a married man, and lay in bed after a fight with his wife, he would figure out that this is how some women behave.

She rounded up the two of them, and summoned the subject teacher at chemistry lab, where practical was going on. More than the possibility of having to repeat a year, he was upset for leaving his teacher embarrassed in front of an outsider. Not that he particularly liked her but for she was his teacher. He always had a certain respect for teachers, maybe for they helped him be a better person, or maybe it was because they filled the void of elders in his life. Or maybe, he felt they weren't treated justly by students and schools. Despite working hard for something that mattered the most – the future of a nation, they were a subject of ridicule and under-paid. *They got too little in return, for what they gave to society!*

They both were then asked to leave the room, and their answer sheets were taken away. In that moment, Shivam had a weird realization. He actually didn't seem to care about failing the exam, or getting a back year. *He had in-fact been failing all along*, and it was a feeling of liberation. He mulled that even if he failed, he can start over again. It was something he couldn't do if he keeps going down the same unidirectional life path, set for him by others. A life of his ways and dreams, was taken away bit by bit since childhood. There were so many other things a person can do apart from studies. He didn't want to be an engineer, or scientist or whatever nerds do. He always felt pressurized studying dull subjects like science and computer applications.

Also, the whole hum-drum made about this thing, him feel like a criminal. And that too *didn't seem to bother him!* He had no shame or guilt, albeit a tad remorseful. He sat there in an empty corridor, imagining for himself an alternate career as a criminal. They were then asked to report at the principal's cabin, where the receptionist asked them to call their parents, and ask them to come to the school as soon as possible. Vaibhav rang up his father first, who probably left right away. Meanwhile, after thinking about it for fifteen minutes, Shivam mustered courage to call up his father. For one, he wasn't sure that he would pick up the call and two, even if he did pick up he won't come. However, he rang him up, and wasn't he right? His father, Tej was visibly upset and refused to come. Although he knew it would happen, yet it broke his heart. He felt alone.

Soon afterwards, Vaibhav's parents arrived. They were very concerned and met the principal right away. What is it about the only child? Whatever rabble they rouse, their parents always seem to forgive them. They tried to calm Vaibhav down, which obviously wasn't needed, as he was already calm. It was Shivam who needed someone to talk to. He soon left the school, without saying anything to anyone. He felt blank on his way back to his uncle Shyam's place, where he stayed.

There was an unusual stillness and peace of mind that Shivam felt. He realized that day, that he actually had no one to turn up to in times of crisis. Not that he had never felt it before, but had never let himself acknowledge it out of fear, fear of knowing that one is alone. He had been harboring false hopes all his life, and felt that he didn't need them anymore. On reaching the house's doorstep, he didn't feel like entering it. It was rather meeting his uncle who was just a different version of Tej, that stopped him. He imagined him making fun of the whole situation, and him in particular, as always. He was in mood for bland humor, and decided it was better to be alone. So, he instead took an auto and went to his classmate and friend Rajiv's home. A spacious and peaceful place, where no elders would bother him with their prying eyes and questions. Rajiv was son of a single working mother, who was at mostly occupied.

Upon reaching there, rang the bell. Rajiv opened the door but didn't say anything, for there was nothing he could say to make Shivam feel better. He then, climbed the stairs going straight to the rooftop, wide open and with a lot of sunshine. 'A better choice definitely!', Shivam said to himself. He laid down on the floor with no mattresses, no pillow, and no sheets. He had never needed them and slept in the sun for straight four hours. Once awake, he liked the peaceful and sound sleep so much, that he decided to stay there for the night as well. In the evening, he listened to some music on Rajiv's desktop, before going back to sleep, slumbering through the rest of night.

Next day, he woke up very fresh, having slept so well after so long. He first took some time to process as to why he was there in the first place, and what had happened the day before. He then left for his Shyam's home, and reached there in about half-an hour. He rang the bell, and Shyam's daughter Himadri opened the door. She was a sensitive girl, and could always tell his mood from the look on his face. She too didn't say anything, as he went upstairs to his room. There was no one else home, as the couple were both lecturers and had gone to college. He didn't feel like doing anything, and there was no one to talk to. Even his mother hadn't called to check on him, and neither did he expect her to.

So, he lay down and recoiled in his bed, staring at the side wall. Then he rolled up, stared at the ceiling and decided it was better to go back to sleep. He got up in the night, and quietly had his dinner. He didn't tell his uncle anything about what had transpired at school. They all looked at him uneasily as it was unlike him, for he always brimmed with energy, no matter how much life sucked. So, the next day when he woke up, he could feel that there was no more sleep left for him to catch up on. He freshened up and went outside to have some bread-omelet at a nearby *thela*, before leaving for Raman's place.

He and Raman wandered around for a while in the neighborhood, before leaving for Vaibhav's place, who lived nearby. Raman gave him a call, 'Hey, me and Shivam are standing outside your home.' Vaibhav soon came out, and they chatted for a while. As they talked, he reassured Shivam, 'It's sorted out. Don't worry! My father has pulled some strings.' As they parted, Shivam didn't knew how to feel - to be happy or sad. *It was all the same again.* He will now have to lead a study-work-marry-die life. Was he dead inside?

CHAPTER IX

Afloat

'Hey, Karun, remember the evening, when we sat on a boundary wall of college. All of a sudden you fell forward, and hit the ground. The high of a whitener, so cool and cheap was unlike any other in the world.' Lokesh said. It was Karun's birthday, their friendship spanning fifteen years, longer than Lokesh's marriage of seven years. As they drove along the road, Lokesh played the song 'Excuses'. Life has moved in very different directions for both, as Karun joined his family business, while Lokesh worked odd jobs to make ends meet.

But the friendship survived, as they continued being close. Sometimes, even their wives get jealous of their bonding. Lokesh's wife Kiki calls, 'When are you guys coming home, haven't you had enough of your girlfriend?' He replied, 'We're on our way back. Will see you soon.' He then turns to Karun, 'Remember my 21st birthday when we escaped death?'. Whenever they're quite high and Karun drives, Lokesh never forgets to mention it. And Karun can feel hairs on his hands rise, every time!

It all began in class eleven in 2006, when both were enrolled in evening coaching classes at school by their parents. The classes had begun two months back, and they both remained strangers, until one day when they met at the watercooler near canteen. The deafening silence post school, and the empty grounds, reminded Lokesh of his boarding days. As he drank water from tap, he heard 'Fool, At least drink water properly!' for he'd spilled some water on the ground. He looked up, only to find Karun standing next to him. The both had a laugh about it and spoke for a while. Once back in the class, they shared the leftovers from lunch, that Karun had brought from his restaurant. This was the beginning of their lifelong friendship.

They came from similar, and yet dissimilar family backgrounds. Both their grandfathers had been farmers in the Hindi heartland of Uttar Pradesh. Presently, Karun's family runs a bar & restaurant in the city, while Lokesh's father is a lecturer in the suburbs. Soon, they were out often, going to movies, exploring places, and sometimes bunking evening classes. Leaving school by the same bus, they got a lot of time together to share their tastes and experiences.

Karun was eccentric and Lokesh was adventurous, though a bit hesitant. They shared same taste in music, food and travel and had an itch for mis-adventure. Lokesh was from 'A' section, while Karun from 'B'. A, indirectly stood for 'Ability', while B stood for 'not A'. A stupid and archaic concept of segregating students in sections, basis their grades in previous years. 'A' section was no play, and no fun, where the students mostly discussed studies, Harry Potter, and going abroad. So, Lokesh soon began hanging out with Karun's friends from badlands of 'B' section.

The school bus didn't go to Lokesh's home town in suburbs, and his school didn't have a hostel. So, he stayed at a private hostel run by a guy called Albert. A close friend of his father, Jeet had suggested the it. Albeit most students were Hindus, on Sunday mornings they'd have bible readings. He didn't mind them, in fact he enjoyed listening to the stories. But, he disliked the twisting of words and interpretations behind verses by Albert. With time, Lokesh came to know that he was a missionary, involved in religious conversion. Albert and his son, during bible sessions at the hostel, would often frantically recite verses, apart from two other students Sam, and Indra - who had their reasons. Sam's family had converted from Hinduism to Christianity, for a monthly allowance of 6,000 rupees. While, Indra was in love with Albert's younger daughter.

It was the worst possible hostel, you could find in the city, e.g., unlike a hostel there was no facility to get clothes washed or ironed, so he'd wash his all-white form by hand. But, like a hostel, going out was restricted except for school, barring exceptions. Just like the boarding school up until class X, the food here as well was borderline bearable. Besides, he couldn't have his fill too. If he ate well, weird looks from mess guy and other students, spoilt all the fun. At nights, the juniors and senior students, would sleep upstairs in a not so large, single hall.

These boarders were mostly from farmer families of nearby villages, who either didn't have relatives in the city, or whose parents were not well educated or aware enough to find their children a better place to stay. Lokesh would often ask himself, 'Did Jeet ever see the place before admitting me here, or he just left after visiting the office? Did he come to the hostel at all? How could he have done this to me?' Meanwhile. Lokesh's direct ways didn't go down well with Albert, and discomfort between them grew.

One day, as the evening coaching class got cancelled, he and Karun went for a movie instead. However, a junior from his school named Kadir, who also stayed at his hostel, went missing. Apparently, he had run back to his home town after school, for he too wasn't fond of Albert's hostel. 'Hi, mam I would like to speak to Lokesh. He is a class XI student attending evening coaching classes.' Albert told the receptionist. He wanted to enquire about Kadir, for he was close to Lokesh. 'Sorry sir, the evening classes were cancelled today. The students had left after school.', she informed him.

Unaware of what had transpired, Lokesh came back at his usual time. Avinash, a kid at hostel walked up to him, 'Please go and meet Albert in his office. He told us to tell you so, whenever you're back.' Lokesh didn't have a good feeling about this. He changed to evening clothes and went to the hostel office. As he knocked the door, Albert asked him to come in.

'Where were you today evening?' he asked Lokesh, who now realized that somehow, his cover has been blown. 'I was watching a movie.' Albert fell silent, for he had expected Lokesh to lie. He had taken away all the fun! After a pause, he said again, 'And why is that?' Lokesh replied, 'My evening classes were cancelled today. I didn't want to come back here, besides I haven't seen a movie at cinemas for some time. Since, I had some time, I decided to go watch a movie.' Albert countered, 'Shouldn't you have informed me?', to which Lokesh replied, 'Would you have let me go if I did?' If you can, I'll tell you the next time.'

Robert didn't expect a confrontation, but a walkover. Lokesh continued, 'I don't like being caged here, this place sucks! What is wrong with going to a movie once in a while?' Albert was furious, 'Do you know Kadir went missing today? And, when I called up your school, you too were missing.' Lokesh had no idea, for Kadir had never mentioned the possibility of running away.' Albert, now called up Jeet to complain, having no idea that it was useless. After formalities and having made his complaints, Albert handed over receiver to Lokesh.

'Why do you have to always trouble me?' asked Jeet from the other end. 'I don't like this place, the trouble you've created for me because I have to live here every day. Sorry if I disturbed your evening time. You can go back to sipping your drink now.' Lokesh said, upset that he was. 'Throw him out of the hostel, Albert Ji!', he could hear Jeet's loud screams from the receiver at a distance. Albert said, 'Lokesh you'll have to leave tonight', leaving him aghast. He requested, 'Please allow me to stay for the night. I need to figure out where to go.' Albert agreed.

What made Albert go easy on him the next day remains unknown, for he called him and said, 'Please be more discreet in future. You don't need to leave the place. You can stay.' Was it Lokesh's vulnerability, or a change of heart, or maybe he was just trying to scare him earlier? *Anyways, it was too bad, that he wasn't going to leave this place anytime soon!*

Thanks to time which never stays still, even that sucker of a year went by somehow. Not that the following were any more fun! And when the results of class eleven were out, Lokesh's father was in for a surprise. However, Lokesh wasn't as he had expected this would happen. Lokesh had failed at an exam in life for the first time, with his Chemistry score of 18/70 in theory. He felt so bad that he didn't even take a bus back to his hometown, and walked afoot all the way, 45 kilometers – starting out at twelve in the afternoon, and reaching home by six in the evening!

Jeet asked, 'What went wrong Lokesh?' to which he replied, 'Haven't I been telling you all this time, that that hostel you put me is not any good.' He then continued, 'You can't sow mango and expect a guava – that hostel is a life sucker! If I'm not happy there, how can I perform? Besides, my classmates who live with family have tuitions. Nothing gets taught properly at school, they neither take the school teachers seriously, nor let them speak. You should be happy I've failed in only one exam.' Leaving Jeet perplexed. As Jeet was pondering about what to do next, AP Tomar a friend who stayed in the city, walked in with his family.

When AP asked, 'What's bothering you Jeet?' He told him about it all, and AP offered to let Lokesh stay at their home for a year. Jeet was relieved and agreed, saying 'Thanks man!'. Lokesh wondered, if Jeet was really serious about him a few moments ago. 'How can he decide about it without asking me?' he pondered. *But he was not the in-charge! He didn't take the calls! Even if it was his own life at stake here.* Soon, Lokesh moved in with them. He got a room on the terrace at third-floor, not a spacey one, but he liked it. Besides, the room had a desktop, so he could at-least keep himself entertained. The floor had a balcony that offered a peaceful and good view of the neighborhood.

Back at school, the scene post failing the Chemistry exam was a humiliating one. Those who'd failed were asked to leave 'A' section and join 'B' section, until and unless one re-took and cleared the exam they failed in. The exams were supposed to be held in the first week after the school resumed, and the results would take another one to two weeks - three weeks of shame! Lokesh decided to act as if he wasn't aware of it, like he does whenever things go wrong.

When some of his pokey classmates nudged him, their words fell on deaf ears. Soon the Principal came to know that a student Lokesh isn't budging, she sent the vice-principal, also their English teacher to the class. She walked in during the Mathematics class before recess, and said, 'It's come to our notice that a certain student refuses to leave this section as per directions. Anyone who's failed must take a re-exam in order to rejoin their section. I therefore, request him to please leave and shift to the other section immediately.'

Lokesh buried his face into a book, not raising it until she left. All his classmates and his teacher stared at him. He didn't leave, and he would never leave. For he wasn't the one to leave, until he wanted to. He is a free bird in mind, if not physically. *He won't ever leave without a fight!* That week, he gave it his all, recalling all his inner strength. When the results were out two weeks later, he scored 48/70.

It wasn't his best, but just enough to keep him afloat!

CHAPTER X

Tassel

The year was 2008, when two best friends, Lokesh and Karun had found a sanctuary in the third floor of former's uncle AP's house, where he'd shifted recently. They could study in peace while listening to songs, play video games and watch steamy videos on the desktop. 'What the hell are you doing?' Lokesh asked as he flinched, seeing what Karun was up to. 'Sorry bro! talk to you later.', he replied in a trance. On screen was playing the latest xxx CD from city market, and soon Karun's face twitched. The champagne showers of Karun's self-satisfaction sickened Lokesh. Though they still laugh about it, Lokesh still says, 'Man, it was weird, and honestly I would've stopped talking to you, if you ever did that in front of me again.'

Since, he was struggling in Chemistry, Lokesh found a tuition near Karun's home. But he didn't have a bicycle on him, so he dusted up an unused one, that belonged to his uncle JP's ten-year-old son Vishnu. Isn't that what he has been doing till now in life, managing. 'Will there ever be a time, when I won't have to?' he asked himself. *He didn't want to be so good at it anymore, adjusting and managing, that it seemed to becomes his fate.* Post tuitions, Karun would oft say, 'Lokesh, let's have some Hakka noodles at the Tejgarhi crossroads.' Across the road, used to be a big hoarding of PC, that they would ogle at. As long as it was there, they needed no more CDs, the imagination was enough. Thinking about it at late nights, their milk shakes would follow hand-shakes! Fourteen years on, they still laugh about it, whenever Lokesh quirks, '*Saat boond aaj!*'

At school, Lokesh continued spending most of his free time in the library. He liked the solitude and satiated his desires of yearning in learning. The empty library, where you could listen to the wall clock ticking, gave a feeling he couldn't find elsewhere in the day, of time standing still and mind working freely. Sometimes, they went to school by Karun's two-wheeler, purposely missing their buses of different routes. Often, taking a detour via the Meerut city clock tower, they'd pass through narrow lanes, where sex workers called on them from rooftops. For small-town, middle-class striplings like them – even this was a rush, given the repressed societies we live in.

Meanwhile, they found a great friend in Anita, a school teacher. Karun liked her, and somehow got her number. Thereon, Lokesh began texting her from Karun's Nokia 1100. While Lokesh liked the rush and excitement, Karun liked the progress he was making. When things were up and running, Karun said, 'Lokesh come with me when I go to meet her today.' Lokesh agreed. Later in the evening at her home, Karun knocked at the door. 'Hi!', she said, as she opened the door with her beautiful smile. Only, that smile was for Karun, not him. Soon, they sat in the guest room, laughing and eating. He saw the love in her eyes, and the lust in Karun's, making him think if he'd done the right thing after all.

As Karun's visits to her place grew more frequent, he'd often ask Lokesh to tag along, trying to avoid rousing any suspicion at either's homes. Lokesh never said no, for he liked her company, over time becoming a good friend with her. 'Hey, you guys have come after a long time. What took you so many days to come?', she complained jokingly. 'We were busy with our lab practical and tuitions lately. Besides, its's been tough for Karun to get out of home owing to strict nature of uncle-aunty.' Lokesh said, explaining on Karun's behalf. He was now officially a *latkan*, a third person that hangs between two lovers. Later that evening, Anita said, 'You too can come alone to visit sometimes, if you want to.' Lokesh looked at Karun, then back at her, and said, 'You mean it?', he asked. She smiled and said, 'Yes, why not. Aren't you my friend?' He didn't look at Varun again, not wanting to see the look on his face. *This word friend can take on complex meanings, when between a guy and a girl, if even one of them has feelings for other.*

Though, he never went alone to her place, sub rosa he wanted to. However, his friendship and his hesitancy got the better of him. Karun would often discuss his relationship issues, and Lokesh would give suggestions, sometimes even texting on his behalf. Karun would sometimes say, 'Bro, you hesitate too much, like a girl. You fear and overthink things, and always need a nudge. You don't lack the courage or will, just lack initiation. If only girls knew you, surely any girl could fall for you. Besides, they love the slim body you have.' Something similar to he'll be told in future by his college roommate, Atharv. Waste of talent, maybe?

Anyways, what really stopped Lokesh was his fear of ruining a relationship, even before it begun. What could he possibly give a girl, apart from some love, more pain and his unresolved issues? Besides, he had no resources, was penniless, had no vehicle or room to take one to. Lokesh had long ceased believing and over time, his regrets and sexual repression had left him in a very complicated place.

Meanwhile, Karun was making progress in the relationship. One night, he told Lokesh, 'I kissed her bro!' As he went on with the details, Lokesh didn't want to hear anymore. Why? He too had begun liking Anita. With time, as their escapades increased, Lokesh began distancing himself from them. It's a surreal feeling when you know someone, while they don't know that you know them! He slowly, stopped going to her place and changed the topic whenever Karun talked about her. 'Hey, Anita was asking why you won't visit her anymore?' Karun asked him one day. 'I don't' want to be a latkan anymore between you guys. I don't want to spoil your fun.', he replied with a smile. Karun smiled back. Lokesh wondered, if he had got a hint of his feelings.

Laying in bed that night, he thought to himself, 'In all our conversations, could she never figure out that I'm the one who schtuped her mentally?' It was stupid of Lokesh. All through, he had known this would happen, and yet he was upset. In his dilemma, he made peace with himself saying, 'Well, she got the best of both worlds – mental and physical passion. What more could I wish for her?'

CHAPTER XI

Partners in Crime

Lokesh had been preparing for his XII boards, when he fell ill. 'The mercury is hovering between 103-104 degrees since last two days. I've severe fever and headache and consulted a doctor, but there's been no improvement.', he told another doctor. 'Here, take these medicines, and come see me after two days.', the doctor said without looking up. It turned out fruitless, and last four days felt like hell. Wobbling in bed, he badly missed the sound of his mother Rukmini's bangles, thinking, 'If she could place wet towels on my forehead, I won't need any medicine.' Having lost faith in allopathy, he decided to give homeopathy a try, and it worked like a charm. In next two days his fever was gone.

That whole week, he never skipped school, for his homestay sucked even more. *When you're down, you're down alone but when you win, the whole world is yours.* Life keeps reminding us in many forms, in sickness, pain, losses, demise, heartbreaks, and what not. We turn humble and grounded, but soon forget move on. *Is attachment a necessity or a luxury?* Are we really social animals or we try to be?

'Lokesh, school will be over soon. We need to find ourselves a college.',Karun said, taking out some prospectus' from a bag. As they ruminated, figuring out where all to apply, he said, 'We will choose only outstation exam centers, as this'll give us a chance to travel more.' Over next few months, they applied to many institutions, ranging from NDAA, AIIIMS, Jumia Milia, BIITS, NIFFT, NIIFT, etc etc. While visiting hometown, Lokesh's father, Ram asked, 'Did you fill the IIT and UP-CEET forms?', 'No' replied Lokesh. 'May I ask why?', Ram asserted. 'I can't crack IIT, and UP-CEET is way below my standard.', replied Lokesh. 'Are you out of your mind? UP-CEET will guarantee you an engineering seat.' To which Lokesh blurted, 'I don't want to be an engineer!' Ram shook his head and left.

NDAA returned his application, citing he was underage. Next, they gave NIFFT entrance exam on an early February, sunny day at a college in Dehradun. Lokesh told Karun, 'Although I didn't attend any of 20 questions from Mathematics section, I'm still confident that I'd make the cut. I was flawless at rest of the sections.' A few months later, with some trepidation, Lokesh punched in his roll number at a cybercafé in Meerut. The slow internet, resulted in a dramatic loading of page, like a curtain falling on stage.

His neutral expression kindled Karun, who bent over to have a look, 'Wait listed, rank 206, general category. In a course of 210 seats, and 50% reservation, how'll you ever get admitted?' Lokesh said, 'I hope I do. I badly want to, and wish nothing more.' Karun knew that if Lokesh is *resolute, destiny makes way.* Lokesh saw the look on Karun's face, realizing that he was upset. He said, 'I'll not be able to join you. Let's do engineering only. 'Separations are eventual, but not permanent.' Lokesh had said at the time. Although he knows now, how Karun would've felt. In hindsight, maybe it'd been better if he'd stayed.

Though he wanted to go NIFFT, it seemed tough given some hundred others needed to drop their plans of joining. Ram had always wanted Lokesh to be an IT engineer, so he decided to give it a try, but only if he could get in BIITS. On the day of entrance exam, Karun abruptly backed out. 'Hey listen, if you don't want to give the exam, at least come with me to Gurgaon.', Lokesh tried cajoling him. 'Sorry, got to go.', replied Karun. Lokesh was left in a fix, and waited for him to change mind. He left alone, 30 mins later than planned, all the buffer time now wasted. The probability of missing the exam was high, nevertheless he gave it a try. Changing buses and autos, in a blend of sad and angry emotions, all that came to mind was, 'No one cares!'. Reaching the examination hall fifteen minutes late, he was denied entry. He first requested, and then begged, but the invi told to take another date. Going back home, 146 kilometers to tell Ram, that he missed the exam wasn't a good idea. He would've asked, 'What did you do with travel money?' *If he had left alone on time, how different his life would've been today?* Something died in Lokesh that day.

Few weeks later, a postman dropped a letter at his home. Ram opened it, and called Lokesh, asking 'NIFFT? What is this letter for?' 'I don't know.', expecting a rejection letter. Ram said, 'Tell me when you come home'. Opening the letter, Lokesh was delighted to see it was for a call for counselling. 'Is it worth it?', Ram questioned. 'As far as I know, I want to go.', he replied. He would've preferred Delhi or Bangalore center, but his rank wouldn't allow it. 'Hyderabad, Mumbai or Kolkata?', Ram said looking at the top three of available centers. 'Hyderabad it is!', he said, as Ram deposited the demand draft. So, Lokesh was set to go to the most premier fashion college in the country. Weird, for he'd never even wore branded clothes, barring Outlaw by Foutons! *It didn't bother him much, nothing does unless he lets it.* Going from a family background of farmers cum government servants to the private sector was renegading in itself.

Once in college, he'd scourge the city with friends for cheap knock-offs to upgrade his wardrobe. The concept of window-shopping was alien to him, a typical middle-class boy that he was from the 1990s. With time, he mustered courage to visit the branded stores, and later departmental stores too. Soon, he rid himself of hesitancy, of leaving a store without buying anything, knowing it's not below dignity to do so. *He learnt to say 'no' after browsing, unless he really liked what he saw.* Owing to a lack of palatable vegetarian food options, Lokesh eventually became a non-vegetarian. He'd often run out of money, by last week of every month, and found his rescue in Golden Leaf, a restaurant owned by Arif bhai, whose revolving credit he'd clear in first week of next month. The place was a lifeline! Golden leaf was like a credit card that he'd max out before every vacation towards the end of semester. When back, he'd got a little extra cash to pay his dues.

Karun visited Hyderabad twice, during his first year and third. In the first visit, he'd stay on for two long months! Back then, his colleagues and even some faculties had begun to think, that he was a student at the college. Lokesh showed him the doors to whitener, smoke, and drink (not sure if he knew it himself!), in short – how to ruin himself. Though studying in separate cities, they'd make short trips in and out. Once, they happened to visit Agra and after seeing the Taj Mahal, disappointment of high expectations hit Lokesh, for nothing is larger than life. *Life is always like this,every time we have high hopes from anything or anyone, the chances are we'llbe let down.* Exceptions are always there, and of all the places, one that did not disappoint him was Golden Temple at Amritsar.

In third year of college, they interned at the same clothing factory of Modern Craft in Gurgaon, staying at a PG near sector 44. In the evenings they'd sit at Machaan, talk about anything and everything in the world. Back then life was full of hope, dreams and infinite possibilities. In between they'd take long road-trips by Karun's motor-bike to Rajasthan and elsewhere.

Earlier that year during a road trip, on the eve of Lokesh's 21st birthday, coming bring from Bhakra Nangal Dam, they halted at a town to grab some drinks. As night fell, they stopped again at a *kohlu*, enroute to Jalandhar. Having boosted themselves with a little *gud*, and having relaxed their sore bottoms after hours of riding, soon they were back on the road. As Karun rode at 100+ kmph, two lights at opposite ends of the road approached them. Taking it for two motor-bikes they rode on precipitously, when each felt something brush against their arms slightly, at both sides of body. Ceasing the ignition immediately, they looked back. What they saw moved them, for the lights weren't of any motor-bikes but a truck and a tractor, each with a missing head-light at either end, towards the middle of road! They had just escaped death, and felt grateful being re-born. It'd take another ten years, for such a feeling to revive, when they'd enroute to Goa.

In November 2020, as lockdown eased, they left for a four-day bike road trip from Bangalore to Goa via Hampi. Leaving Hampi in morning, they stopped after Dharwad to grab some snacks. While discussing further route and which hotel to book, Karun pointed, 'The fuel needle is nearing emergency. Let's get the tank filled at first petrol pump that comes along the way.' The night was about to fall. While in the city, they had decided against stopping at a petrol pump owing to the rush. Assuming there're always a few petrol pumps along the highway, they didn't bother. Little did they know, that the route that they'd taken for shorter time could make them 'late'.

Fifteen kilometers inside the forest, the networks were down. Kiki was getting upset over something, but Lokesh couldn't hear her. After another ten or so kilometers, the signal bars disappeared entirely. By forty-five kilometers, the fuel level had dipped to almost nil. With nothing in sight except boards warning against wild animals, both their hearts began to sink. A handful of villages they'd cross, were small even by standards of a village, with no shop carrying petrol! It was only close to 8 PM, and people were nowhere in sight. Ever since taking the highway # 67, they couldn't recollect a vehicle passing by them.

Soon, the engine stopped firing intermittently, and their motor-bike began to halt now and then, sputtering in between. It luckily pulled up near a small restaurant, with people in sight. 'Yay! We're going to live today.', exclaimed Lokesh. Parking the motor-bike there, they returned to road and tried to stop a car, that came out of and disappeared into nowhere. Few minutes later, another vehicle approached. Lokesh was unsure of help, but anyways waved his hands. The car stopped and the driver pulled down his window screen, and asked 'What's the matter guys?' Lokesh spieled the whole thing post-haste. 'Where's your bike?', 'There, nearby that restaurant.' Lokesh pointed towards roadside, assuaging the inmates' concerns.

They got in the car, a little relieved but anxious too. 'What if they screw us?', Lokesh could see the question in Karun's eyes, and silently replied with his eyes, 'Do we have a choice?'. They were dropped after ten to fifteen kilometers, at the nearest market of Ramnagar, where they could find petrol at shops. They were just in time, because within next ten minutes, the shutters were down. They took lift from another car on their way back to motor-cycle.

Back on road, they got the tank filled at a petrol pump Ramnagar, to avoid another derailing. The route ahead was replete of broken, and incomplete roads, where the roads began to disappear into mud hills. *Welcome to India, where the roads aren't laid, and we ride into jungles, losing our way!*

After crossing half the jungle, the roads were finally back in sight, with phone batteries nearly drained, and signal bars still suffering from erectile dysfunction. The dense forest, and eeriness of empty roads, made Lokesh reminiscence of their night road-trips in Rajasthan. Until Panaji, their motor-bike and a Tharr trailing them were the only two vehicles to be seen on that road. With drinks on table at the hotel room late at night, they said, 'Cheers! Welcome to Goa.', feeling grateful.

CHAPTER XII

Poison

'Hey, what's your poison?', a double entendre we often come across. If she ever asked me, I'd say, 'What wasn't poison in your absence? Your presence is my nectar.' There's no way to know, if she ever would. On a serious note, a poison is something that kills. Either slowly or rapidly, quietly or mercilessly, partially or completely – but it does kill for sure!

Poison surround us, it's in our food, water, air, minds and hearts, for whatever gives us life, takes it too. Some poison tends to stay – like the deadly poison of unfulfilled desires, choking our necks like a snake, its potency depending on the elements of both, the poison and poisoned. For someone, who is conditioned to being poisoned, a little by little, day by day, even a deadly poison might be ineffective. But, there are some poisons which are exceptional – so strong, and definitely fatal. Yet, we all are bound to die by one, and we have our favorites. So, the right question to ask someone is, 'Which poison would you prefer?'

When I was a kid, there was a poster on a barber shop's wall of my home town. If I remember correctly, it was an ad by a cigarette brand Tills Lifestyle. FYI, the ads for this poison did not always feature a cancer patient. Anyways, a handsome guy and a charismatic lady, stood in conjunction near a red helicopter, with snow-clad cottony mountains in the background. 'Can I ever be this guy?', I used to ask myself. I would often imagine myself sitting in a sprawling garden in front of my huge mansion, fenced with trees. I imagined having a few luxury cars, and a secret room in the basement, where I'd be inventing things, no one had ever imagined of. Too big a dream, maybe not. Too little actions, maybe yes. When did I stop dreaming and stopped believing? When did I stop being a kid? When did I change?

'Romil is dead. He commited suicide on the railway tracks.' I got Watsapp'ed by a relative. He'd also sent a few gory pictures and videos. Pallavi, my wife came rushing from bedroom, and the look on her face gave it all away. I was shocked and muttered, 'There he lays in two pieces, my cousin and childhood friend.' Just like Kabir who never returned from his trip, Shyam who got electrocuted at a flour mill, Anil who never recovered from illness, Kamakya who died of cancer, Vikram who died in an accident, and many others, he was gone to soon. In one of the videos, I could see his upper half move a little, while the other half lay still. How differently we'd behave if we knew someone was to leave us soon? What would we do differently? Would we be more kind towards them? And how do we know we're not next? Isn't life uncertain?

As children, we met during vacations at my paternal village in Saharanpur, where our families stayed in adjoining houses. We both, and sometimes his younger sister, Sonam used to play on the rooftops. He had some good cricketing skills, a left-handed batsman, who was hard to beat. Besides, he was fun and rugged. 'How did he end up like this?' I wondered. As if she read my mind, Pallavi said, 'Apparently, he was stressed for some time and used to fight with his father. Today afternoon had another fight, and he marched to the railway tracks nearby his field, throwing himself in front of an upcoming train.' What a waste of talent?', was all that I could say. He had commited suicide. *At what moment does one give up?* Maybe, I will never know, or will I?

Like many others do, he'd left behind a wife, kids and ageing parents. Is it selfish to die? Don't we all leave one day, in one form or another. Isn't death the ultimate truth. Is his father happy now? Whatever the fight was about, could it have been more important than his son's life? With Romil gone, will he be able to ever forgive himself? Meanwhile, more messages kept pouring on Watsapp. One read, 'Romil was alive for thirty minutes before breathing his last.' Another read, 'There was no point of taking him to the ambulance. What would have been saved? It was already too late!' Another one said, 'He was sorry for what he'd done, wanted to live, and to be taken to a hospital in an ambulance.' I buried my head in my hands. When is it too late before we do some serious damage? Is there a way to know, if we're going to blow it before we do? It isn't possible to always know the consequences of our actions. All I know was, that he'd died by poisoning of being misunderstood.

Some say relationships define us. If that's true, I am screwed for life. And maybe even after life or many-after lives. I never had a real one, for no one made me feel, except one. I've always been a blunder, and everyone's blundered with me. I've been too aloof and everyone's been aloof with me. Later that night, my father, Kishan called me out of the blue. He said, 'If there's something bothering you, then let me know.' It's wasn't hard to guess, why he had called. Anyways, it was the only high point of our relationship, for in a moment of sadness, there was a touch of love. What else, did I ever ask for? Next day, he sobered up and we went cold again. So much for some concern!

Isn't life in itself a poison? Is the death of dreams and end in itself? How can there be no one who believes in me? I'm not a bad person. I just need a chance. Why is the world such a diplomatic place, where no one ever really shares their thoughts or experiences? Is there someone who can be really counted on? We all know the answer, and yet delude ourselves. Is this why gods and gurus exist? Am I poisoned? Guess so, but I can hold more! The poison of toxic relationships, by blood or otherwise.

Kishan and my uncles are three siblings, though once there used to be four of them. She had left the world at a tender age of sixteen. Surprisingly, I came to know of it, when twenty-nine years old, and when I asked my mother, Rashi, 'What happened to her?', she replied after a concealing pause, 'She wasn't keeping well.' It felt made up, for there had to be some details. Why no one ever mentioned her? Why there is no picture, or memory of hers in his paternal house? It was like, if she had never existed. Men like Kishan, the orthodox ones are such hypocrites.

A three-year-old me saw Rashi, scream and shout fervently, as Kishan along with two other friends, tried to calm her down. It looked like a scene out of an exorcism movie. She spoke in a weird voice, in an angered tone, and seemed too powerful. As she pushed three men back with one hand, I sat outside the door, thinking only one thing, 'What if something happens to her? What will I do?' From that day on, I was extra protective of her. At nights I would often pretend to fall asleep keeping my eyes closed, when I really wasn't. I wouldn't go to sleep, until she did. Sometimes she would sneak out the bed and go to Kishan's room. I would be awake, until she came back and slept next to me.

When in high school, I asked her, 'What happened that night?' She told me, 'Someone did some black magic on me.' I never knew if she was serious, will I ever? I believed her back then as a kid, but I don't anymore. Given she's depressive, I'd rather think of it was a mental breakdown. I can't ask her now, for we don't talk anymore. Everyone is so taciturn, everyone's a master at hiding, that sometimes I wonder if I'm being 'loose lips.' Anyways, even if we talk, we never really talk, for it's like playing an old record. I guess there's a subtle difference between mystery and secrecy. While, one attracts and other repels. Besides, if secrets can't be shared, where's the scope of intimacy. Isn't lack of thereof, a poison?

What is a dose of daily poison? A person, who sucks the life out of you, leaving us less, every time. Not being true to oneself, and staying where we don't belong, like being stung by a scorpion, every time! We keep finding alternatives, a new poison every time, until one sticks. What if you're already poisoned? A poison be an anti-dote too. -+-

I consider myself guilty, of giving those pills to Pallavi. With a pale face, she said, 'I'm worried, for I haven't had my chums as usual this time around.' I said, 'That happens sometimes, doesn't it? Why're you worried?' She'd felt that she'd somehow conceived, despite us trying otherwise. 'I'll bring the pregnancy test kit today, after office. There's nothing to worry about.' I tried calming her down, and left home. Our son Vikram was only two and a half at the time, and we weren't doing well financially. Neither was our married life certain, for only a few months back, there loomed a possibility of divorce. She was right to be worried. I believe in love with no filters, and never liked rubber. Isn't rumpy pumpy all about feels? I prefer to not call it 'love-making', if it's not with a lover, or for love.

Maybe, all I ever tried were basic ones, and maybe I should've been more experimental. But that was my problem, so I'd not have her take birth-control pills, barring exceptions when I came inside. Everyone loses themselves sometimes, I'm no different. And I feel sorry for the times we don't, for what is the point if we can't lose ourselves? In the evening, coming out of the washroom, she handed me the kit that showed a pink line, validating her. I congratulated her, but she pleaded with me, teary eyed, 'Do something!'

I'd never want for a life to end, that too when it just was coming into one. But, at the same time I could not see her like that. I was caught in a real dilemma. I tried to convince her, but did she ever listen to me? She'd rather induce stress and bring me misery – mental, physical, spiritual, financial or otherwise. This time too, she had her way, and I let her have the final word, for it was after all her body. But, it is something that I'll never come to terms with. She drew an invisible line, that'll always keep us apart.

CHAPTER XIII

Dead-End

When did you last laid back and look up at the sky? When did you last felt at peace and did nothing? The best things in life are free, and the best feelings are inexplicable. But, in a complex web of society we humans create and blend in, complications cannot be ruled out anyway. We thrive on dilemma, love the undefinable, and chase the unsolvable. If something's out of our reach, we desire it the most – sometimes actually achieving it!

Nature - the ultimate balancing force of universe, gives everyone, the same quota of experiences. Notwithstanding our unique histories, geographies, chemistries, biology', stations and situations in life, we all share the same emotions. The timing, occurrences and intensities of events may vary, but we go through same feelings, over and over again. As centuries turn to millennia, the drama repeats itself, albeit with a change in backdrop. Then, all is wiped out and we go back to fresh beginnings. *The Mandelbrot set, and its thumbprint of god* – is the perfect example of how we can find the story of Ouroboros play out within our lifetimes, for each part is a whole.

In the quest to make our lives easier, have added to our uneasiness. In a quest to make our lives better, have traded it for worse. The only thing we ever have on us is, so intangible and so limited – our time. And yet, we trade it for money and we call ourselves free! All ideologies from communist to capitalist, from socialist to monarchist, from imperialism to oligarchies, have failed. *Ideologies don't work, Anarchism does!* We are free-willed, and chains make us weak, limiting our potential. If only we could trade differently, how many talents would be utilized? How many people could lead more fulfilling lives, not having keep on doing the same things we get bored of. *Humans are not machines!*

The institution of marriage, too needs a major overhaul. *The concept has become so archaic and useless, hindering growth of our civilization.* Do we need to marry to find love or make babies? Do marriages guarantee sexual monopoly? Have our minds become so numb to new ideas? When our ways of living have changed in all spheres, what are we afraid of – women's unrestrained and unbounded sexuality? And what about different laws for different religions and regions, for the same humans? Isn't divorce rate over 40% in UK and US? Don't some religions allow polygamy? Does Indian divorce rate of less than 1% mean, our social and legal structure makes us continue to suffer in silence? I bet, for it's not just love that keeps us together. If we're really inextricable, do we need a paper or social approval!

O are we scared that we call property, never really ours, and of no use to us when we die, could be relished by others? Why not instead build better old-age institutions, given we're so scared of dying alone? So pious and loyal we are, except only we slip, when given a chance – hiding in cars, hotels, resorts, movie theatres, flats, dark rooms, messengers and where not. A few cannot change the system – those on the top don't care, and bottom ones are voiceless. It's only the winds of change that can alter status-quo, and they're already gathering storm.

It's hard to get by without love, only if I understood that earlier. When no one thinks of us, we need to think about ourselves. If a marriage doesn't work out, does one keep on trying to make it work only to find, that the best years of life have gone by? Or do you call it quits? How do kids affect one's decision? As I go against the grain, there's nothing more fulfilling. I shall screw what's screwed me, and be an original. Isn't anything legendary an original?

'Hey, come here for a minute. I need to talk to you.' Kishan said. Sitting on a folding bed in the lobby, he asked, 'Son, when do you plan to get married?' I'd never considered it before, so this question out of nowhere unsettled me. I said, 'Not for at-least another three to four years.' I've never even had a girlfriend; how could they presuppose that. He continued, 'Everyone must marry someday. Tell us what do you want?' I replied, 'If I have to do it, I'd prefer an educated, working girl, who's well-travelled with a life of her own.' I wanted to tell them about my pyramid of desires, but chose not to. For where could they find a woman –

so winsome, that I could drown in her eyes
so divine, that I could spend every day of my life with
so calm and patient, that could handle my transgressions
so irresistible, that I could make love to her day and night
so transformative, that partakes in my dreams and aspirations
so effortless, who gets my highs and lows and accepts my flaws
so heavenly, who knows of my dark places, fears, and yet isn't afraid

A few weeks later, my mother, Rashi said on phone, 'Son, just go and meet her once.', as she cajoled me to go and meet Pallavi, as customary for arranged marriages. 'Mummy, you know I don't want to get married right now. I'm not settled, so how will I take care of her.' She said, 'If you don't like her, just say no.' I reiterated, 'You're not getting my point here. Anyways, I don't want to break a girl's heart by rejecting her for no fault of hers.' She persisted, 'Your father has already given his word, don't make him look bad. Just go.' I had no choice, I felt at the time.

Few days later, before we left, my best friend Tarun called. I didn't pick up, for I was screening him over a recent squabble. That was my second chance, but I toyed my destiny that day. On our arrival, Pallavi's father said, 'This visit is just a formality, for we've already decided.' as her mother Savita laughed, and when a girl's mother behaves so, a night-mare awaits. I looked at Kishan's discreet face. Pallavi walked in timidly, with shaky hands, and I mistook her disposition for nervousness. When nobody left or asked us to, I greeted her and asked, 'What did you study in college?' 'I'm an arts graduate from DU.', she replied. She indeed was, but without ever stepping into a college, pursuing studies by distance mode.

'I like watching English movies and series. What do you like?', 'I prefer Bollywood movies.', she replied, adding, 'I like Honey Singh's songs.' She might be fun, I thought. Her sister-in-law' kept sitting next to her as if glued, and I assumed, that she might be shy. *Assumption is the mother of all screw ups!* After a few more assumptions, I assumed that she seemed 'okay'. I didn't have a girlfriend, and my parents wouldn't stop bickering until I'd marry. So, I walked outside the room to Kishan, and he asked, 'So?', and I said, 'Yes.' In the repressive societies we live in, conforming is the norm.

I see doublethink when people with failed arranged marriages, fix marriages for their children. *It's called 'tying the knot' for a reason.* On the way back, I told Kishan, 'She doesn't know anything!' I'll never digest what he said, 'Isn't that a good thing.' Both my parents were well educated, at least I used to think so. How then could they turn out to be so orthodox? I started doubting if I did the right thing. After a few of reluctancy, and Pallavi wanting to talk on phone, my doubts were confirmed. Slowly – layer, by layer I knew she and I would never be compatible. I told her so, and she cried. She didn't budge. Whenever I'd visit home on weekends, I'd ask my parents to re-consider and cancel the wedding. Rashi would pass the buck to Kishan, who would say, 'What if someone did this to your sister?' I had no answer to this, but I did say it'll ruin me, it'll be the end of my dreams. They didn't seem to care. I thought of running away or relocating elsewhere, but I didn't want to hurt Pallavi.

A relationship sans trust is like a plate riddled with holes, that stains and drains. I told her all wrongs I'd done in my life, and about my being careless, irresponsible and broke. She was upset but only said, 'Whatever's in past is past. My parents would blame me, if the marriage falls apart.' She wasn't happy either, for I wasn't price charming either, and she was not even given a choice. I stopped taking calls from her and my family. Nothing changed, except my parents tried to visit me in vain. When I finally spoke, I told them – if I leave her someday, you'll be to blame. In the due course of our married life, I did come close to that, each time I ended up having a baby, each time I went a little deeper into the ground.

The next I went to her home, Savita put a gold chain so tight it gripped my neck. Pallavi was six years old, when her paternal aunt Savita, adopted her. Her birth-mother had three daughters in a row, hoping for a son each time. Savita only son longed for a sister, so it worked for both. Pallavi is a little reticent about those times, and I get why. It wasn't the best childhood, she'd wanted. Savita often says, 'Our fortunes changed for better after Pallavi came to us.' When do my fortunes wake up? It's already been seven long years! Nobody seems to care when you're in mess, even if they created it. Until recently, I was taking personal loans just to get by, forget any savings! *You can't dream when you're poor. And day dreaming, seems like a stuff of dreams.* Poverty comes not in only one form of currency, for one devoid of love is the most impoverished.

A wrong marriage can wreck people, for some people are just bad for your health. You can't think or do anything, but you can't run away either. What is the price of ruining a life? What is the punishment for ruining in life? This is what happened to my pyramid of desires, I had a woman –

soirksome and loud, that I often cringe
so rancorous, that I'll be smothered aeon
so violent, that it my soul is replete of scars
so repulsive, that her words cut deep into me
so incompatible, that it kills dreams and hopes
so difficult, that it's hard to be happy and myself
so iniquitous, that my dark side never saw the light

In today's ever-evolving world, being technically challenged is a major disability. As the adage goes – if you teach a man, you teach a man, but if you teach a woman you teach an entire village. It was unfair to not send a daughter to college, not teaching her to ride and drive. Why obsess over sons? Why not treat daughters at par? But, patriarchy rules, thanks to women who don't complain.

When Pallavi was carrying our firstborn, Atul, Rashi kept guessing, if the child was a boy or a girl. It used to trouble Pallavi much, and I'd try to comfort her, 'I just want both of you to be safe and healthy.' So, when Pallavi was carrying our second child, Amita,

I flatly told Rashi, 'Mummy, this time it's most probably a girl. Aren't you satisfied with one grandson?' She smiled greedily, and I hated it. The day Ichcha was born, I called Rashi from the hospital, 'It's a girl.' She paused briefly, before saying 'Congratulations!', and then adding, 'It doesn't matter if it's a boy or a girl.', she didn't sound convincing, in fact it seemed as if she expected something else, trying to come to terms with the facts. Why can't women, respect women? Why have notions that a daughter is a drain of wealth?

Printed by Libri Plureos GmbH in Hamburg,
Germany